✈ Praise for ✈
The Martian Alliance Chronicles

Anthologies
CLOCKWORK UNIVERSE: STEAMPUNK VS. ALIENS
A Clockwork Alien
TWO HUNDRED AND TWENTY-ONE BAKER
STREETS – *All The Single Ladies*
UNIDENTIFIED FUNNY OBJECTS 3 – *Live at the Scene*
TEMPORALLY OUT OF ORDER – *Alien Time Warp*
THE X-FILES: TRUST NO ONE – *Sewers*
UNIDENTIFIED FUNNY OBJECTS 4 –
Support Your Local Alien
OUT OF TUNE 2 – *Red River Valley* (coming 2016)
alt. SHERLOCK HOLMES: NEW VISIONS OF THE
GREAT DETECTIVE – *A Study in Starlets* (coming 2016)
UNIDENTIFIED FUNNY OBJECTS 5 (coming 2016)
HUMANITY 2.0 (coming 2016)
ALIEN ARTIFACTS – *Alien Epilogue* (coming 2016)
WERE- – *Missy the Were-Pomeranian vs. the Masters of
Mediocre Doom* (Coming 2016)

Alliance Rising

The Martian Alliance Chronicles 1 - 3

GINI KOCH

This is a work of fiction. Names, characters, places, incidents, and dialogues in this book are of the author's imagination and are used fictitiously and are not to be construed as real. Any resemblance to actual events or persons, living or dead, is entirely coincidental.

Alliance Rising
The Martian Alliance Chronicles 1 - 3
Published by Gini Koch at Smashwords

Copyright 2015 Jeanne Cook

The Royal Scam first published by Musa Publishing October 2011
    Second Edition 2015
Three Card Monte first published by Musa Publishing October 2012
    Second Edition 2015
A Bug's Life first published 2015

Editors: Mary Fiore and Veronica Cook
Cover Artist: Lisa Dovichi

ISBN: 978-1-51889-9188

Gini Koch
http://www.ginikoch.com

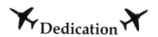**Dedication**

To all the fans who said this is their favorite series of mine, the Martian Alliance thanks you for your support.

Acknowledgments

Many thanks to the ever-awesome Lisa Dovichi, Artichoke Head Creative, my fantastic agent, Cherry Weiner, and the fastest and best beta reader in the West, Mary Fiore. Love to my family and fans for supporting me in everything I try –
you're the best in the galaxy!

The Royal Scam

BOOK 1 of the MARTIAN ALLIANCE CHRONICLES

GINI KOCH

"Princess Olivia! Are you sure this will work?" my lady-in-waiting gasped out as we hurried along the walkway by the docking bays. I was looking for a specific ship, one that could get into space fast and jump to hyperspace even faster.

I took her hand and pulled her along. "Positive. You have the wedding dowry from Prince Ignatius?"

She shoved the bag of galaxy-wide gemstones into my hand. "I double-checked. They're all in there."

The Captain of the Guard was on her other side. He held her other hand. "You're still set on going alone, not taking us with you, my princess?"

"Positive, yes." I looked around. We were definitely not alone, and even though I had a long cloak on and the hood up, covering most of my face, we hadn't been speaking softly. I knew at least some of the space folk in this area had heard us.

"You've cut it close," the Captain said. "The wedding is tomorrow."

"Whatever." I spotted what I was looking for—a small, sleek spaceship. It was more elegant than most of the other ships in the bays. It reminded me of a little silver bird. I recognized this class of ship—Strikers.

Strikers had been created during the Purge. They were still among the fastest and most nimble spaceships flying these days, difficult to trap, harder to catch. Best of all, the ship appeared ready to depart. A human male and what looked like a walking toad were fiddling around in the way all spacers seemed to right before liftoff.

I walked quickly to them; the others followed.

The man turned, and my throat tightened. He was tall, handsome, with blue eyes and light brown hair. He

The Royal Scam

was in tight pants and shirt and was clearly all wiry muscle. He also had on a double laser belt and high boots, common to spacers from Mars. Just standing there he radiated masculinity. His eyes narrowed as we reached him.

"I need your help," I said without preamble. "I need to get off-planet immediately. I'll pay you well."

He looked us up and down. "Where are you headed?"

"Old Earth."

He snorted. "That's a long way away...Princess. I know why you want to go there—no extradition to Galaxy Core planets. But it'll cost you. A lot."

"How do you know who I am?"

"Like the rest of the Andromeda Royal Family, Princess Olivia is tall, fair, and beautiful. And, like her three sisters before her, about to be married to a Prince from Diamante, where they grow them rich and ugly."

"There are plenty of attractive women on Andromeda."

"Yes, two of them are here before me." He nodded at my lady-in-waiting. "They make sure the closest retainers resemble their assigned royal here, too. And who else would have the captain of the guard along? You're incognito, somewhat, but he's not." This was true. The Captain was in his full uniform. "Price of flying with us is high, especially under the circumstances."

I handed the bag to him. "This should cover it."

He looked inside and raised an eyebrow. Then he handed the bag to the big, walking toad, who'd joined us. "Take a look." He looked back to me. "I'm the captain, so if this checks out, fine, we'll do business with you."

More spacers and dock workers were nearby. I was certain most had marked what we were doing and some had heard what we were saying as well.

The toad emptied the contents into his large, webbed hand. He closed his eyes for a few long moments. "Real."

The captain nodded. "All three of you—get on board. Now. I think we have company."

I didn't turn around. It was likely the Royal Guard.

"Just me." I turned to my lady-in-waiting and hugged her. "You stay here. Try to comfort my parents as best you can."

She hugged me tightly. "You've been the best friend I've ever had—"

"Hush." I let her go and hugged the Captain as well. "Take care of each other."

"We will. Godspeed, Princess." He stepped back and gave me the Royal Salute only given to the Andromeda Royal Family. I curtseyed as appropriate to the Captain of the Guard, then the ship's captain and the toad hurried me on board.

"Places everyone, now!" the ship's captain snapped. "You come up to the cockpit," he added to me.

"Of course." I tossed my cloak off and followed him. I was in a one-piece fighting suit, so it wasn't like I was stripping.

We passed a dreamy-looking woman. Her hair was almost white-blond and floated around her head. She smiled serenely. "All is in readiness."

"Good."

She followed us to the cockpit. The captain went to his seat, and I sat behind him. A humanoid man sat in the co-pilot's seat. Well, humanoid if you didn't count that he had wings as well as arms and legs, and that his head was more bird-like than human.

The birdman turned to me and blinked slowly. "Good to see you." A traditional greeting between strangers from his home world.

I gave the traditional response. "And to see you."

"Strap in, all crew," the captain said over the intercom. "We have military company."

"Right on schedule," I murmured.

"Cut the chatter," the captain said. "We're lifting off." He didn't ask for clearance, which was wise.

The ship blasted off amid a lot of shouting from the flight controllers. Their concerns and orders were ignored. We had to avoid several small planet flyers but we did so with ease.

"We've hit escape velocity," the birdman said. The ship shuddered as it shoved its way through Andromeda's atmosphere.

"And here's the Royal Armada, right on cue," the captain muttered.

The captain tuned the radio to the universal communicator link so we could hear what was being said from the command decks of the other ships. Ships from Andromeda and Diamante were trying to surround us without harming the ship, because I was on board.

"Don't hurt them," I said urgently. "They're only doing their jobs."

The captain shot me a dirty look over his shoulder. "Oh, of course not." He turned back, muttering under his breath, while he calibrated coordinates, flipped switches, and pushed buttons to ready us for the leap into hyperspace.

Good spacers were part engineer, part astrophysicist, part pilot, with speed, dexterity, and good reflexes. Great ones knew how to pull it all together and go with their gut reactions. They also made it look simple. I knew the calculations were complex, and if the wrong switch was flipped or the right button pushed too early or late, we'd all be space dust. The captain was barely looking at what he was doing, other than the computer calibrations.

He grunted with satisfaction. "Maneuvering into position to jump."

"Almost ready," the serene woman said.

"Need to wait," the birdman said. "We need the right option."

"Running out of time," the captain said calmly, as he locked coordinates.

"Unidentified ship, we demand you return Princess Olivia to Andromeda immediately, by decree of King Oliver of Andromeda and Prince Ignatius of Diamante." King Oliver was speaking from the planet.

I leaned over and hit the communications button. "I'm sorry, father. I love you and mother very much but—"

"Now," the serene woman whispered.

"Agreed and ready," the birdman said, just as softly.

A shot headed straight toward us from a Diamante ship. There was no way any ship would escape this direct a hit. I screamed, as loudly as I could, but I could still hear people shouting on the other ships. The captain hit a button, and everything went quiet.

Time slowed down.

When I looked straight ahead, all I saw was the laser beam heading for us, the armada, and the real outline of this ship.

But when I looked out of the sides of my eyes, I could see something else, superimposed over us. A duplicate of this ship, only a little bit larger. As the beam reached this image, the image shattered and exploded.

Our ship, the real ship we were inside, shimmered and jumped to hyperspace right as the shot "hit" the counterfeit ship. Myriad pieces of destroyed spaceship were my last visions of Andromeda's solar space.

The next few moments were spent feeling compressed. There was nothing to see but blackness. If the calibrations were wrong, this would be the last thing any of us would know — suffocating blackness.

A few moments more of the feeling of suspended death, then my stomach turned inside out and back again, proving we'd made a successful jump.

The windshield blacked out to prevent anyone from being able to see what we were flying past. In the olden days they'd lost many a spacer to blindness or madness, before some unsung genius thought to ensure the "no peeking" rule be built in automatically for every space-worthy ship.

We were all quiet for a few long moments. The serene woman opened her eyes. "All clear. It's a sad day on Andromeda — Princess Olivia is dead."

I breathed a sigh of relief. "So, can I relax?"

"Yes." Ciarissa smiled at me. "You can go back to being you."

"In a second," Roy said as he hit some more buttons, flipped switches back, spun dials, and checked calibrations. My stomach did another set of flips, meaning we were out of hyperspace. The windshield becoming clear again was also a clue.

"Ciarissa, are we still clear?" Roy asked as he took the ship off of the hyperspace automatics and put it fully under his and Doven's control again.

She closed her eyes again. "Yes. Doven made us disappear at the perfect moment. All witnesses believe that our ship moved erratically into the line of fire and so was destroyed by a Diamante shot. I find no questioning minds. No one on Andromeda or Diamante doubts that Princess Olivia and the crew who were trying to help her escape are dead."

"Are any more mind readers searching for Princess Olivia?" I asked.

"No." Ciarissa smiled at me as she opened her eyes. "Welcome back, DeeDee. Nice job. No one seems clear on who the captain and crew were, Roy."

He nodded. "I have the best crew in any galaxy. Doven, can you handle flying solo for a bit?"

Doven ruffled his feathers. "Of course."

"I'll keep him company," Ciarissa said. Doven looked pleased.

Roy and I left the cockpit and I heaved a sigh. "What's your pleasure?"

He grinned. "I like the real you."

I raised my eyebrow. "You're sure?"

"Well, if the real you is my little voluptuous redhead, yeah."

"Not so sure about the voluptuous part, but the little and redheaded is indeed me."

Roy grinned. "Trust me on the voluptuous."

I shifted and heaved a sigh of relief. I'd been Princess Olivia for three months, which was a long time to play pretend. It was an even longer time to be away from Roy.

He put his arm around me. "So, want to tell me about it?"

"Not yet." I still had to rearrange my mind back to my own. I'd liked Princess Olivia a lot, meaning it was harder than normal to leave her behind. Almost as hard as pretending I didn't know who Roy and the others were when I was in character.

Good shape shifters were, at our cores, the best method actors in the galaxy. We not only shifted mind and body but the best of us could, once shifted, maintain that indefinitely, even while sleeping. Basically, if we believed we were whoever, or whatever, we were imitating, so did the rest of the galaxy.

One of the easiest ways to trap a Shifter involved catching them "knowing" someone the person they were impersonating wouldn't or couldn't. In addition to giving the Shifter away to someone paying attention, it affected their overall control as well. Our history was littered with Shifters who'd made one small mistake that proved fatal. I had no intention of joining their ranks.

Because of this ability and the risks of being found out when shifted, we learned to keep the real us hidden, deep inside, under different mental, physical, and telepathic layers of protection. Once shifted, those of us with the highest levels of power, training, and control could access the reality of who we were, but it was close to impossible for anyone else to do so, even the most powerful telepaths.

The return to true self took little time externally, more time internally, and much more mentally. When a Shifter was deep undercover, all you had to remind you of who you really were was what we called the Golden Thread — the link back to where you'd hidden your true self.

Some Shifters lost the Thread and never found themselves. Some cut the Thread, to remain who they'd turned into. Sometimes the Thread was cut for love, but in many cases, it was cut to allow the Shifter to remain hidden permanently.

Not that there were a lot of us left, experienced, hidden, or otherwise. Not after the Diamante Purge. I needed to keep my mind on going back to being me, though, so I tabled old angers for another time.

I was a pro at this by now, but even for me I needed safety, security, and relaxation in order to make the full return to myself.

Roy knew. He led me to our quarters, then waited while I adjusted back to me, inside and out.

It took a little longer than normal, about an hour, before I was fully back. I looked in the mirror and spoke the Mantra of Self.

"My name is Danielle Daniels. My friends call me DeeDee. I was born on Seraphina and carry part of it within my body and soul. I'm a member of the crew of a ship known only to said crew as *The Hummingbird*. My life is my own, my loyalty is to those I love and those I serve."

"You forgot, 'and I'm Roy's girl.'"

I laughed. "That goes without saying."

"Missed you, babe," he murmured as he pulled me into his arms. "You have to kiss anyone while you were on assignment? Or anything else?" He was always worried after every job, which I found extremely flattering. Between the two of us, the one more likely to get suggestive offers was Roy.

I chuckled. "The beauty of impersonating royalty is that no one expects them to put out before the wedding night." I snuggled closer. "Besides, I have the best kisser in the galaxy right here."

Roy did his best to reassure me that he hadn't lost any skills while we were apart. He was still the best—at everything.

He stroked my arm as we lay together in the afterglow. "You hungry?"

"Only for junk food. Good eating on Andromeda, but they really keep a rein on anything unhealthy, at least for the Royal Family."

"We stocked up on all your favorites."

"Knew I loved you."

We got dressed and went to the galley. Bullfrog was there, still holding the bag of gems. He grunted at us. "Good pay. Better than last time."

"Well, Andromeda royalty pay well. Besides, each assignment is tougher than the last, in that sense."

Roy sat down and pulled me into his lap. "Fourth princess in this family line to do a runner and get 'killed.' And yet the Diamante Royal Families aren't suspicious?"

"We do good work."

"You mean you do," Roy said.

"We're following your plan."

"Which only works because of you."

I shrugged. "Shape shifting isn't extraordinary if you're born with the talent."

"True. But you do more than shifting your shape," Roy said, as he stroked my back.

He was right, of course. Every Royal Family worth its crown had telepaths around. Fooling them, and everyone else, took more than just changing your shape. You had to change your mind. Modestly spoken, I was the best there was at becoming someone else.

"Well, I couldn't blame Olivia. Prince Ignatius is a toad, and I don't mean a toad like Bullfrog."

Bullfrog rolled his eyes. "No insult intended, I'm sure."

I ignored him. "*And* she fell in love with the Captain of the Guard. I mean, who wants to stand in the way of true love? I have to give Olivia credit—her guy's a hunk and a half." Roy grumbled, and I went on quickly, "But you have to hand it to Andromeda—they have the best ability of any planet to get out of debt creatively. And the best track record."

"Approaching Roulette," Doven said over the intercom. Roy sighed as we stood up. I stayed with Bullfrog while he headed back to the cockpit.

"Nice haul," Bullfrog said when we were alone. "No compunction from anyone about stealing from Diamante?"

"None. Andromeda's my kind of planet." So was Roulette, an entire planet devoted to gambling, betting, and other related pursuits. No extradition, either. Though we weren't going there to hide—we were going to collect our winnings.

Willy joined us. He was our ship's engineer and usually stayed below decks, just in case. "Missed you, little girl," he said as he seated himself next to Bullfrog. We all strapped in for landing. "What was it like?"

"Like the other times."

I liked the King and Queen of Andromeda. They didn't want to make their daughters marry jackasses or jerks. But Andromeda wasn't a rich planet, resources-wise. So, King Oliver had, long ago, been more than willing to go in on what we called the Royal Scam. We had a lot of scams, of course, but this one was near and dear to everyone's heart.

Roy's in particular.

Diamante, on the other hand, had a set of Royal Families that made the Old Earth Borgia's from millennia ago look like the kindest saints in the galaxy. They were rich, one of the richest planets in the galaxy. Yet they longed for more—they wanted to be considered legitimate monarchs, not just rich merchants who dressed up and put on crowns.

They longed for other things, too. Old Earth had finally given up the idea of genetic purging before they'd expanded out to explore and help populate the rest of the galaxy. But the Diamante Families didn't like certain races and planets, and they'd spent a dozen years proving that, back when most of us on the crew were children.

Of all the planets out there, I hated Diamante more than any other.

I felt the ship shift, just a little, meaning we were coming into range of Roulette's sensors. Doven's talent again. Altering the ship's general shape and changing the call letters was child's play for Doven, especially after making the ship "disintegrate" in front of thousands of witnesses.

Roy wasn't exaggerating — he had a great crew.

We landed, and all nine of us gathered together. Roy always had us do this before disembarking, so he could brief us and make sure no one gave him or Ciarissa a bad feeling. Roy trusted Ciarissa's telepathic skills, but he trusted his own gut even more.

Dr. Wufren, Tresia, and Kyle joined the rest of us by the main cabin exit. Dr. Wufren gave me some round, red and white discs. Of course, being a telekinetic, he floated them to me. They spun around, doing a pretty dance in the air.

I put out my hand, and the discs landed neatly on my palm. "Gaming chips from the Joint?"

"From my last visit," Dr. Wufren replied, his watery blue eyes twinkling. "I was unable to exchange them for something more useful."

"Because we were too busy running away after you got caught cheating," Roy reminded him.

Dr. Wufren shrugged. "One must keep one's hand in, my boy. As you well know. DeeDee my dearest, will you please arrange to exchange these lovelies for something lovelier still?"

"Of course."

"I could do it," Kyle offered.

Dr. Wufren chuckled. "I'm sure you could, my boy. I'm sure you could."

I laughed. "Trying to steal my job, Kyle?"

Kyle was a mini-Roy. Smaller all the way around, but still obviously Roy's younger brother. He flashed me the family grin. "Nah. Nice to see you back, DeeDee. Bro's been a pain to be around. I've had to hang with the doc and Willy to stay out of the line of fire."

"Kyle even helped me in the galley." Tresia tousled Kyle's hair with one of her pincers. "Never thought a human could really help much, but I have to say, he's good." Since Tresia was a humanoid arachnid, this was quite a compliment. "Kyle's not exaggerating. Roy was more than a little...testy...while you were gone."

"Yeah, right," Roy muttered, looking embarrassed. "There was a lot going on."

I linked my arm through his. "Oh yeah, tough guy? Why don't you tell me all about it while we see what our payout is?"

Ciarissa handed me the cloak. I took a risk, wearing it off the ship right after Princess Olivia's "death," but it was part of how we proved the scam had worked. I'd made sure the cloak was expensive but not all that rare—anyone with enough credits could have purchased it, from a variety of planets.

"Fine. I want everyone other than DeeDee and Bullfrog to stay on the ship and be ready to run at a moment's notice," Roy said. "We may have to make a fast exit, and I don't want to end up stranded or captured because someone's off gambling. Or anything else," he added with a glare for Willy and Dr. Wufren.

Everyone gave the standard good-natured grumbles, but no one argued too much. We'd done this drill often enough. The downside to Roulette was some of its laws, particularly those that affected Espens. Ciarissa and Dr. Wufren would need to wear special headpieces that blocked their tele-talents. Technically, as a Shifter, I should be wearing an elaborate set of body armor. As if. I shifted, just a little, all on the inside.

Kyle, Willy, and Tresia could all go into Roulette without issues, but since we weren't here for fun, they were better off staying on-ship. Besides, Roy was protective and did his best to keep his little brother out of harm's way. Sure, we didn't succeed all that often, but still, he kept on trying.

The ramp lowered, and the three of us walked down. We were greeted by a flying robotic attendant, typical for Roulette. "Names and purpose?"

"Captain and partial crew of the *Hyperion*," Roy said. We hadn't been on the *Hyperion* for years, so it was unlikely to bring up anything negative out of the planet's central computer. "On Roulette for a short visit with an old friend."

The robot flew around us. I was tense but fairly sure the robot couldn't sense it. Whether it could or not, the robot didn't make any issues. "Two Earthers, one Polliwog." I assumed Dr. Wufren and Ciarissa had honed some skills while I was gone. I knew my internal rearrangements had shown me to be an Earther, as opposed to a Shifter, but the only true Earther we had was Willy — Roy and Kyle were Martian. And, Martians were right after Shifters on the popularity rolls these days. "What is the makeup of the crew which remains on board?"

"Two more Earthers, one Arachnidan, one Quillian, and two Espens," Roy replied briskly. "If they leave the ship, the Espens will wear appropriate gear." Doven's talent was extremely rare, and like my status, we didn't list it on the books.

"You may proceed. Enjoy your stay on Roulette and may luck grace you."

Interestingly to me, Espens weren't hunted or even feared. However, they didn't run the galaxy, either, and considering eight out of ten Espens were telepathic or telekinetic of some kind, this was surprising. Ciarissa and Dr. Wufren had never explained why Espen functioned as it did. I figured they were either all peaceful at their cores, or else there was a larger scheme in place Espen's leaders didn't feel they needed to share.

I kept a casual lookout. "No one's taking undue interest."

A variety of holoscreens hung along the walls of the spaceport, creating a bank of moving, life-like visuals streaming in from every planet in the galaxy. Many of them showed a continuous loop of the firefight we'd just left. "...the horrific explosion ended the short life of Princess Olivia of Andromeda," an announcer's voice said. "Next up—is Andromeda's royal family cursed? Our investigative reporters give you the real news."

"Think they'll create a problem?" I asked Roy quietly.

"No, standard media reaction," he replied in kind.

Roulette had excellent public transportation of all kinds—didn't want anything to slow your getting to a gaming facility. We had a regular bookie we used, but never for payouts from this kind of job. Those who placed a big bet on a political figure's nuptials or death tended to garner a lot of interest from Galactic Enforcement.

Instead, I went back to work. The cloak was serving a double purpose—I could shift under it in crowded areas, and I could also shift the cloak with me, if I was in seclusion. I could also change the cloak's color as needed. Roulette had great security, but there were always ways around it, and we knew them all.

By the time we reached our first casino, I'd shifted to look similar to Tresia, though I ensured I wasn't an exact duplicate—why leave her on the ship if I was going to just have "her" exposed here?

Casinos were equal species opportunity locations, but many seemed to get more of one type of crowd than another. The Web, therefore, catered to those with extra appendages.

The hardest part about shifting into an Arachnidan was remembering which arm to use for what activity. If I'd needed to officially say goodbye to Roy and Bullfrog this could have been a problem, but gathering bets was simple—whatever pincer was closest to the cash was the appropriate choice.

Conveniently, once "in shape" I didn't have issues walking—the body was the thing and I didn't have to learn or relearn how to use my new parts. Sadly, I still had to look in some kind of reflective surface to ensure my shift was accurate. Happily, my two funky, backward-knee-bending legs and six bony arms were all in place, pincers clicking away like I'd been born in a cocoon. I resisted the urge to wrap the cloak fully around myself—Arachnidans wore cloaks as adornment, not for protection from heat or cold. I reminded myself that I found Tresia quite attractive, as Arachnidans went. Besides, Roy was already elsewhere.

I did the herky-jerky walk that was deceptive in its ability to cover ground fast, and reached my first payout window. Long line, but not too bad.

"Your payment in casino chips or planetary currency?" the Arachnidan behind the counter asked. Most casinos hired Arachnidans for their casino cages, not just the Web, because those extra limbs were helpful and no one wanted one of the many pincers to close on any part of their body. Pound for pound, Arachnidans were the strongest beings around.

"Currency, thank you." My voice sounded similar to Tresia's—higher pitched, melodious.

The Arachnidan behind the bars was male and apparently a fan of Tresia's vocal pattern. I got an appraising look. "Busy in a few?" he asked as he carefully counted out my winnings. Clearly Tresia was his type. Pity she wasn't around to enjoy the flirtation.

However, there were flirtation rules. I raced through what Tresia had told me while I watched him neatly stack and straighten the bills. "I'm flattered you're interested in my schedule."

He slid the bills through the small opening between us. Per Dr. Wufren, casino cages, regardless of planet or historical age, were all pretty similar—lots of bars keeping the average gambler away from all that money. "I enjoy sharing company while I dine."

Oh. Wow. He was asking me out to a meal. This was a big deal. Clearly my cashier was either a lothario or he was really smitten. Either way, this wasn't good. Folks tended to remember someone who'd stood them up. Or turned them down cold.

I spotted a big Arachnidan at a nearby craps table. I dropped my voice. "If I can escape my mate's notice, I would be pleased to join you." I looked pointedly at the big guy, who was busy waving around chips in two pincers, drinks in three others, and rolling the dice with the last set. "He can be so...protective."

The cashier looked as well. He was about half the other Arachnidan's size. "Ah. I would not want to upset a joyfully mated pair." He slid my money to me quickly.

"Oh." I did my best to sound disappointed. "Well, thank you for the compliment. Good day." I took the money and herky-jerked my way over to the big guy. I sidled up next to him. "Hey, can I get a kiss for luck?"

He grinned, tossed the dice, put down one drink, and wrapped that arm around me, bent me back, and planted one. Fortunately, we kissed without tongues involved, mostly because I kept my lips clamped shut. I'd had to kiss an Arachnidan romantically in the past. If you think eight limbs is odd, try three separate tongues, two of which are very sticky.

"Winner!" the dealer shouted.

My "mate" was happily distracted by this. "Heading to an Easy Eights table," I said, pretty much to no one. He nodded, his focus back on the dice. I wandered off, confident he'd never remember me and that the cashier would be doing his best to forget me.

A big clutch of a wide variety of beings stood around the Easy Eights section. I mingled into a group that had several Arachnidans taller than me. A dark alcove was nearby—very small, but large enough for what I needed.

I stepped into the alcove, altered the cloak's color just slightly, and went to Earther form. I pulled the cloak around me now, ensured the hood was up, moved back through the crowd, and left the casino. No one followed me; no one tried to stop me.

Headed to the next casino on the list and did the process all over again. Over the course of the next twelve hours, I shifted from one look to another. This kind of shifting was easy and didn't need the same dedication a full impersonation required. Men, women, humanoids—I covered all the major planets and all the major races. No bet paid out higher than ten thousand credits. I hit the Joint early, lest I disappoint Dr. Wufren, and added his old winnings to our new haul.

The biggest risk we had was conversion. Planetary money is fine, and space credits are nice, but nothing travels like precious gemstones. The Andromeda Royal Family understood this well, but Roulette's goal wasn't to send you home rich beyond your wildest dreams. Theirs was to have you give all your winnings back and then some.

The risk with conversion was that the only one of our crew who could determine real from fake was Bullfrog, and it was hard to hide a Polliwog anywhere or anytime, unless you were actually on Polliworld itself.

So, I gathered payouts and slipped them to Roy. Roy handed them off to Bullfrog, who made

conversions in almost as many places as Roy, and the crew had placed our bets. Difference was, while I got a variety of small payouts, Bullfrog collected a larger amount before he went to make the trades. His cover— as a runner for the Polliworld Underground—seemed to work well. No one liked to run afoul of organized crime from any planet.

Twelve hours is a long time, and we allowed ourselves a couple of breaks. But the faster we could collect and convert, the faster we could get off this particular rock and head somewhere safer. No extradition on Roulette didn't mean no prisons.

Roulette's prisons were nasty and even though I'd gotten out, I didn't want to press my luck and go back. Ever. Sure it had been a long time ago. Sure Roy had rescued me. Sure the entire situation had ended up changing my life in a good way. I still didn't want to make a return visit. Call me unadventurous.

We were almost done. Roy, Bullfrog, and I sat together at a small café, comparing experiences, tallying payouts and conversion rates, and ensuring our plan was still working. The news feed blathered on about Princess Olivia's "death." I hoped she was okay. I always tried not to get truly attached to any of our clients or marks, but working with Andromeda so often made it difficult, at least in the Royal Family's case.

"One more stop and that's it," Roy said, checking receipts.

I wasn't an Espen, but I got a funny feeling. "Which bookie?"

"Not a bookie, straight casino bet. From The Jewel of Roulette."

"That's a Diamante Families casino, isn't it?" The funny feeling got worse.

"Yes." Roy eyed me. "What's wrong?"

"I'm not sure." I focused on the news. They were talking about Princess Olivia's death, but the Diamante Families were being mentioned. "Listen."

We all did. "Sounds like the Families are trying to insinuate foul play," Bullfrog said finally.

"The shot that 'destroyed' the ship was from a Diamante vessel," Roy countered.

"Which would be why they're trying to shift blame." I considered how King Oliver thought. "Roy, your fourth daughter in a row has 'died under mysterious circumstances,' each one before she could marry a Diamante prince. Let's say Diamante gets suspicious. What would you do?"

"Try to shift the blame onto them," Roy said without missing a beat. "Go for the whole 'your vessel's shot killed her' sort of thing." His eyes narrowed. "You think that's what's going on?"

"I think King Oliver is easily as smart and sneaky as you are, Roy, so yeah, I think so. And I'd also guess that someone in the Diamante Families is wondering if this is all an elaborate set up."

"Go for whoever takes out a big payout?" Bullfrog asked.

"Probably."

Roy shook his head. "Were you the only one taking Andromeda payouts?"

I snorted. "Hardly. At some casinos I had to wait in line."

"So, we need to collect this one from the Jewel. If we don't, it'll be as suspicious as if we do."

"If the Diamante Families create enough issue, the bookies might hold on the payouts," Bullfrog pointed out, sounding worried. Not that I could blame him. The risk of monies being held was a big reason why we got our payouts immediately whenever possible.

I thought on this. "Okay. I have a plan. I want to take Bullfrog back to the ship."

"Why?" He sounded offended. "I'm the best we have in a fight after Roy."

"Because you're carrying all the money, my beloved toad. I really want what we have safely tucked away before we deal with our last payout."

Roy shrugged. "I've learned—never argue with DeeDee. She always wins."

"Let's hope my record stays intact, then."

"I don't like it," Roy said, for the eleventh time by my count.

"You never want to let me do anything," Kyle muttered.

"I prefer to have you on the ship. So someone I can trust is there, just in case."

Both Kyle and I gave Roy derisive looks. "You trust everyone, more than me sometimes," Kyle said. This was probably true. Kyle was the least experienced of anyone on our crew, and Roy didn't want anything to happen to him. Ever.

"Not only are you my family, my responsibility, and part of my crew, but we're the last of our line," Roy snapped. "I promised to always protect you. If something happens to me, you're the only hope we have."

I could see the old argument forming. From the first day I'd met them, Roy and Kyle had argued about their true responsibilities—to each other, to Mars, to the galaxy. Roy, despite his protestations to the contrary, was truly a traditionalist. Kyle wasn't.

"We don't have time for the trusty 'the blood of the true rulers of Mars runs through our veins' speech, Roy. Besides, Kyle, like the rest of us, has it memorized."

"If I'm our only hope, then maybe I should be better trained."

Kyle was trying a new tactic. Must have been from spending time in the kitchens with Tresia. Arachnidans were good with coming up with alternate ideas. She said this was because if someone said "on the other hand" a lot more options opened up when you had six as opposed to two.

I was impressed, however the new ploy wasn't working on Roy. "You're trained. You also don't need to be in any extra danger, just for the thrill of it all."

"I'd argue—or at least let Kyle keep on arguing—because I've missed this for the past three months, but we need to get moving. Don't worry, Kyle. It took years for your big brother to let me do things without his worrying."

Kyle snorted. "DeeDee, didn't I tell you what he was like while you were...on assignment? He's like that from the moment you're out of his reach until the moment you're back."

Roy looked embarrassed and worried, but at least the potential argument seemed averted. "Fine, whatever. I still think this is a really bad idea."

"I don't. I spent three months with them. And that was my fourth visit. I understand how the Royal Family thinks."

"But if we do what you want," Roy protested, "then we'll screw up their payouts, too." That the Royal Family had retainers placing the same bets we did was a no-brainer guess.

"You worry too much."

We left the ship and went through the same robotic docking check as before. I'd shifted to look like a Polliwog while Roy and Kyle were arguing, so it appeared we were still a team of two Earthers and one big, walking toad.

The robot passed us through, and we headed for our final destination. We reached the Jewel in a few minutes, during which time I had to resist the strong urge to catch and eat every flying insect around. Roulette had a good share of them, too. But most Polliwogs "ate" in private when they were off their own world. Besides, regardless of form, I found insects to be unpleasant coming in, going down, and coming out.

We went inside, and I stepped into the first bathroom we came to.

Bathrooms weren't allowed to have surveillance in them, for a variety of reasons, all related to personal privacy. That daintiness didn't apply to exits and entrances, so I took care to be in a stall that didn't provide a clear shot from the door. I shifted again, then hung out for a while, until another Polliwog came in.

Fortunately, they liked to gamble and their home world was close by. I saw some webbed feet in the next stall, and I exited, looking human. I checked in the mirror. I was back to being Princess Olivia, with a few key differences.

I glided out of the bathroom and headed for the betting cages. No one appeared to take an interest in me, possibly because I still had the cloak on and the hood up. I didn't want to draw a crowd until I had our money in my hands, so I waited to take the hood off until I reached the head of the line at the payout cage. Like most of the other casinos, the line was long.

Bettor's ticket passed through, no reaction from the Arachnidan behind the counter. Oh well, I'd planned for that. I counted the payout. Exact, no issues. I turned and left the cage.

The Jewel was the biggest and busiest casino on Roulette. I preferred the Palace, but I was biased toward owners I didn't loathe. The Diamante Families did casinos right, though.

The Jewel glittered. Every surface the decorators could put something shiny and reflective on was so adorned. It wasn't the kind of look anyone should have in their home, but for a place that carried the tagline of "You'll Go Home Be-Jeweled" it worked.

It was one of the more crowded casinos, not just in terms of beings inside, but in terms of available floor space. The only areas with plenty of room around them were the cashiers' cages. There wasn't a lot of flash around these cages, either.

I wasn't sure if this was to discourage gamblers from cashing out, or because the flashiness would distract from the surveillance focused on the money. I bet on them both, but I was cautious that way.

Kyle raced up to me, looking excited. "Oh my Gods!" he shouted. "You're that dead princess!"

The sounds around us changed a little. Not everyone had stopped gambling, talking, or drinking, but some had, because the noise level went down.

"Uh, no. No I'm not." I ensured I blushed. I also kept my voice at its lowest natural level.

"You are! Everyone thinks she's dead, but you're right here!" Kyle was effectively drawing a crowd. Beings of all kinds surrounded us. Their expressions ranged from mildly interested to excited curiosity. Most were clutching gaming chips, some were smoking their plant of choice, many had drinks in what were or passed for their hands.

"I'm not her," I muttered, but loudly enough to be heard by those nearby. I tried to shove through the rapidly forming crowd, but others were now insisting I was indeed Princess Olivia.

Kyle had "stopped" me right under a bank of holoscreens, all of which were blaring different planets' takes on the Princess Olivia story. There were a variety of fingers, claws, and other appendages pointing back and forth between me and the screens.

Security took an interest, along with some men in dark suits who looked like they routinely gave the go-ahead to kill puppies while ordering their breakfasts. Diamante Families enforcers, for certain.

"Come with us please, miss," one of them said as he took my hand in a strong grip.

"No, I'm not that princess." I tried to pull away, then looked down. "I get that a lot, though."

"Right." The man holding me clearly wasn't buying this. I looked around—the other enforcers weren't buying, either. "Let's go. You've lucked into an all-expense paid trip to Andromeda."

I sighed dramatically. "You're making a mistake." I said this as loudly as I felt I could safely get away with and not make the enforcers suspicious in the wrong ways.

Some of my audience seemed to agree with me. Most didn't.

"She's here! Princess Olivia is really alive," Kyle shouted from the back of the crowd. "Glad I got my money already!"

He was really doing a great job of inciting to riot; there was a nasty vibe coming from the crowd. The smokers were puffing more strongly and quickly, drinks were being sloshed about, and the sounds were all along the "I want my money anyway" lines.

"Come on," the enforcer said, giving me a little shake. I flipped my hair around more than his shake warranted.

"No! This is a case of mistaken identity!"

"*Sure* it is," someone shouted. Not Kyle this time. "C'mon, Princess. Tell us how you fooled everyone. Everyone but *us*." The crowd was fully into the show and needed no further prodding. Everyone I could see and hear murmured their agreement.

"I can prove it," I said. I made sure my voice carried to the back of the crowd. I looked around at the crowd. "You want the proof I'm not that princess?" Everyone indicated they did, some loudly.

"Fine," the enforcer said, clearly humoring me. "Prove it."

"Ah, we need to be in private."

He laughed the kind of laugh that has no humor in it but does have the risk of imminent pain behind it. I'd heard laughs like this before. Nine times out of ten, they were coming from someone on the Diamante Families payroll.

"You'll be happier," I told him.

"Sure I will be. You'll prove it here. Now. Or we're going to the spaceport." The crowd backed him and demanded the proof, too. There were some news crews shoving toward the front.

I looked around, giving the news teams time to get into position. "Okay. You asked for it." I took off the cloak and let it drop to the floor. I wasn't in a dress or a fight suit. I was in pants and a blouse. "Really, you're sure?"

Why not ask one last time, for dramatic effect?

"Now," the biggest enforcer growled. My appreciative audience, which no longer included Kyle, but absolutely included a variety of holographics aimed at me, made noises of agreement.

"Okay." I smiled for the cameras and dropped trou.

We headed for open space. Sometimes it was nice not to have an official destination. Once we'd jumped in and out of hyperspace a few times to ensure we had no clear trail to follow, Roy and I left Doven and Ciarissa in the cockpit and headed to the galley.

Bullfrog and Dr. Wufren were counting the money again while Kyle, Tresia, and Willy watched. "I don't like to take paper cash, but I suppose planetary bonds are acceptable," Dr. Wufren said.

I shrugged. "I didn't want to take any more time than I had to."

Bullfrog chuckled. "You spent your time well. The payoff from the Jewel to keep you from taking your humiliation to all the news media who weren't already on site doubled our take from all our other payouts combined."

"Good payday or not, let's not do that again," Roy muttered. "I don't like you exposing yourself for all the worlds to see."

"That wasn't exactly 'myself,'" I reminded him.

"True enough," Kyle said with a snicker. "But I think Roy wishes you'd used another model."

"Hey, I wanted to look impressive." Crowd reaction to my "exposure" had imitated my reaction to seeing Roy naked pretty accurately—gasping and drooling. "Besides, you should have seen the looks on the goons' faces. There was a lot of crushing envy in there, right after complete embarrassment."

Roy blushed, which was something of a rarity. "Can we stop talking about it?"

Ciarissa's voice came through the intercom. "We've received a very encrypted message that bounced through several planetary systems to reach us, Captain."

"Read away, Ciarissa."

She cleared her throat. "Congratulations and many thanks. As always, it's a pleasure doing business with you. Please accept this bonus for going above and beyond the scope of our agreement to ensure our continued safety and longevity."

"Signed by?" Roy asked.

"No signature, Captain. The bonus is a set of Royal Absolutions, good for use on any planet in the galaxy. A dozen, to be exact. They are registered with our private account on Espen."

We were all silent. To paraphrase an ancient saying, this gift was a price above rubies. And diamonds. And even planetary bonds.

Roy finally broke the silence. "Think King Oliver knows what we're really up to?"

"He thinks like us, so yeah. I also think he knows he's not our target and never will be." I was also pretty sure that King Oliver knew who Roy really was, but that wasn't something to worry about, now or later.

Andromeda hadn't been part of the original Martian Alliance, but they'd always been sympathetic to the cause. And King Oliver had schooled on Espen, where, back before the Diamante Purge, all the best royal families had sent their bloodline. He'd been a year or so behind Roy's father, but I was positive they'd known each other.

"Good enough for me," Roy said. "Good work, everybody. Let's relax. At least for a little while."

We sailed through space, waiting for the next job. We had a longer wait for retribution, but we'd all accepted that a long time ago. For now, it was enough to re-count the money. After all, it's the simple things you treasure.

BOOK 2 of the MARTIAN ALLIANCE CHRONICLES

Three Card Monte

GINI KOCH

"Interesting news from Roulette," Dr. Wufren shared with us, his watery blue eyes twinkling, as we all sat down to dinner.

"And from Polliworld," Bullfrog added, as he grabbed his plate from one of Tresia's pincers.

"Is this paying news or just gossip?" Roy asked.

Doven's feathers ruffled. "Why does the news need to be paying? Don't we still have plenty left over from our last job?"

Our last job had been a complicated con for the Andromeda Royal Family. As far as I knew, we still had plenty left over.

Everyone looked expectantly at Roy. He grimaced. "You know, we're not just supporting ourselves. We're helping to run an underground resistance."

Kyle rolled his eyes. "Here it comes, DeeDee," he said to me in a stage whisper. "The 'Martian Alliance Speech' again."

Roy gave his little brother a dirty look. "You, of all people, should care."

I patted Roy's knee. "It's okay, oh captain, my captain. We're all one with the cause."

The others all nodded or murmured their assent, most with their mouths full. We were all focused on restoring the galaxy to what it had been before the Diamante Families had taken over, but empty stomachs were a more immediate need.

Bullfrog grinned, always unnerving because giant walking toads having lots of teeth made most of the other humanoid races nervous. Long tongues were one thing – teeth like any other carnivore in the galaxy were another. "I think the news might be both."

"Both what?" Roy asked. He was really testy. I had no idea why. I ran through possibilities: he and I hadn't had a fight, Kyle hadn't done anything foolhardy, no one we liked had recently been listed as dead, maimed or incarcerated, and there were no Diamante cruisers anywhere in sight.

Sure, we were in the middle of nowhere, space-wise. We'd learned a long time ago to take our time between big jobs. Maybe it was boredom.

"Both gossip and potentially paying," Bullfrog replied.

Dr. Wufren nodded. "But we can wait until after dinner to share."

"No, go ahead." Roy sounded resigned.

I checked everyone else out. No one else appeared upset. Until I looked at Doven. Because he was a Quillian, and so half-man/half-bird, it was hard to tell when he was emotional unless his feathers were ruffled. And ruffled they still were. Just a bit, and he flattened them when he caught me looking at him.

So Roy and Doven were fighting? This was unusual to say the least. However, Dr. Wufren's next words moved the Roy and Doven issue down to second place for my attention.

"Monte the Leech has sold part interest in the Palace and is personally opening a new casino on Polliworld."

It was hard to turn the crew of the *Hummingbird* speechless, but this news did the trick. We all stared, open-mouthed, at the good doctor—except Bullfrog and Dr. Wufren himself, both of whom looked smug about having been the ones to break this galaxy-shaking news.

Roy recovered fastest. "Why?"

"You want the official reason or the real one?" Bullfrog asked.

"Both."

"Per the press releases," Dr. Wufren said, "Monte's done so well with the Palace on Roulette that he wants to expand and bring the excitement of live gambling to the world that likes it best."

"That sounds reasonable," Tresia said. "He could open one on Arachnius, too. I believe we're second in terms of overall planetary adoration of games of chance."

Bullfrog snorted. "The doc left out a key piece of information. Two, really."

"Which were?" I asked.

Ciarissa smiled at Dr. Wufren. "You do like to make a statement, don't you Fren?"

"When I can, my dearest. When I can. As our noble Bullfrog has pointed out, the press reports are avoiding two key pieces of information. First: Monte sold that part ownership of the Palace to the Diamante Families."

"Willingly?" Roy asked tightly.

"Who knows, my boy? However, the second bit of information held back is that Monte's co-owners on dear Bullfrog's home world are the Polliworld Underground."

We were all quiet again, thinking. Kyle broke the silence first. "So? What do we do?"

Roy grinned. "We go visit our old friend to congratulate him on his new business expansion and see where we can get in on the action."

Once dinner was finished, Roy set a slow course for Polliworld. We'd jump to hyperspace after everyone had slept. Some spacers would let their crews sleep during a long jump, but not Roy. He wanted everyone awake and alert when we jumped, in case anything went wrong. It was one of the reasons he was a great captain and leader.

Standard procedure when wc were simply cruising through space was that Roy would take one shift in the captain's chair and Doven the other. On rare occasions, Kyle was allowed this honor. At least, Roy acted like it was an honor to be the only person awake watching a lot of nothing from the cockpit.

Doven took the first shift. I watched him and Roy closely — something was still wrong between them.

I waited until Roy and I were in bed, in part to ensure no one else would hear. The biggest reason was that I enjoyed seeing Roy naked, and didn't want to risk triggering a "storm out of the room" reaction.

Not that anyone would blame me for wanting to see Roy, dressed or otherwise. He was tall, handsome, with blue eyes and light brown hair, and was all wiry muscle. He was dressed like normal, in tight pants and shirt, with a double-laser belt and high boots, which was what most spacers from Mars wore.

Roy radiated masculinity even when he was asleep — even more so as he undressed. I drooled a little, but that happened regularly. Seeing as he was ready and willing to again consummate our relationship, I decided the question could wait.

It waited a good long while, emphasis on long. And good. Really, great. As always.

"So, what's going on with you and Doven?" I asked as we lay together in the afterglow.

"Nothing."

"Right, pull the other one. I can tell. Doven's giving off signs and so are you. I want to know what happened. And I'm willing to keep asking you for the foreseeable future."

Roy sighed. "We've been arguing."

"Gosh, I don't need Ciarissa's, or any other telepath's, help to guess that. What about?"

"Funny you should mention her. Ciarissa, as a matter of fact."

That was weird. "Why?"

"Doven thinks we've been working her too hard."

"Have we?"

"Not as far as she, I, or the doc are concerned."

I considered this. "Did Doven make a move on Ciarissa while I was on Andromeda?"

"No."

"She knows he likes her. Doesn't she? I haven't talked to her about Doven, but I mean, come on, she's one of the strongest telepaths in the galaxy, if not *the* strongest. Why doesn't he just tell her he wants to be more than friends?"

"You know, you feel free to have this romantic discussion with my first mate and navigator. As far as I'm concerned, he's questioning my command decisions without legitimate cause and I'm tired of it."

I knew when to let something drop. I snuggled closer and stroked Roy's chest. He relaxed and was asleep soon.

I was wide awake. Like me, Doven was one of the last of his kind. Not the last Quillian, but among the last Quillians with what they called Shaman Powers. If it flew, Doven could alter its shape, anytime, anywhere.

The Diamante Families had done their best to wipe out the Shaman branch of the Quillian population, just as they had with shape shifters like me. I wasn't sure how many were left, but Doven and I were both high up on the extinction list.

Sleep wasn't coming. I slipped out of bed and pulled on a flight robe. Calling it a robe was kind of a joke, since it was more like a baby sleeper, complete with feet. However, it was made out of absorbent, lightweight material that conformed to your shape, meaning Doven, Bullfrog, or Tresia could wear one if so desired. Flight robes made running to airlocks or to patch hull breaches a slightly more modest proposition.

I trotted up to the cockpit. Doven was in the captain's seat, looking quite alert. He turned his head. "Can't sleep?"

"Nope." I settled into the first mate's spot. "What's wrong?"

"Nothing."

Nice to see he and Roy had both practiced that clever response.

"Right. Will it shock you that I already extracted the argument details out of Roy?"

"No."

"Why haven't you told Ciarissa how you feel about her?"

His feathers ruffled. "This isn't your concern, DeeDee."

"The captain and first mate of this vessel are both upset with each other. That affects me and the rest of the crew. We're heading to Polliworld and I don't want you and Roy not paying attention to something important because you're both too busy being angry with each other."

"We'll deal with it."

"I'm sure you will. You know, Ciarissa's a telepath. You can't seriously think she doesn't know that you like her."

Doven had wings as well as arms and legs, and his head was more birdlike than human. He clicked his beak and glared at me, in the way that birds of all kinds and from any planet seem able to manage — the "I could do terrible things to you if you only knew" look. Cats and birds, they really had it down in terms of glaring ability.

"I know how powerful she is."

I took this admission to its fullest conclusion. "Ah. So you think, because it's clear you're madly in love with Ciarissa and she's never said, 'let's snuggle in my cabin' to you, this means she's not interested."

Doven's feathers ruffled to the point where I wasn't sure if he was going to flap his wings out or not. His wingspan was impressive, and it was far wider than the cockpit area. If he flapped, he'd hit me. And I was pretty sure a part of him wanted to hit me.

But he pulled himself together. Literally. The wings tucked back neatly behind him, the feathers settled down, and the glare was now directed at deep space. "Correct."

"You know, sometimes a girl expects the guy to make the first move."

"And sometimes 'the guy' understands that his love is unrequited." Doven turned his head toward me again. "But even if all 'the guy' receives is friendship, he still cares about his friend and doesn't want her harmed simply because she refuses to tell her captain no."

"What is Ciarissa saying yes to that you don't think she should be?"

Doven shrugged his wings. "Everything Roy asks her to do."

I sat with Doven for a while longer. We didn't talk about Ciarissa or Roy. Instead I asked him to tell me a story about his world and how it began. He was a good storyteller, and I liked hearing about each planet's olden days, before the Diamante Families had decided the galaxy was theirs and the rest of us only got to play in it if they wanted us to.

A good story can give you many reactions, but if the teller wants you to go to sleep when the story's done, well, if they're good, you get sleepy. Doven finished. I yawned widely and trooped back to bed.

I considered my options and kept the flight robe on. It was unlikely Roy was going to have time to be amorous before his turn at the controls. I got back into bed and snuggled next to him. I woke up briefly when he got up for his shift, but otherwise, I slept soundly.

Everyone ate breakfast and dinner together on the *Hummingbird*. It was Roy's rule, and I liked it. We were a family. Sure, we were put together from the cast-offs and fugitives of the galaxy, but we were a family nonetheless.

Either my bugging them had gotten Roy and Doven to talk, or they'd both moved past the issue, because they seemed at ease with each other today.

Which was good, because we had to jump to the Pollisystem. Not all solar systems were named for one of their worlds, but Polliworld was the only inhabited planet its sun had, so had scored the name.

We strapped in. Sometimes Ciarissa and I went to the cockpit with Roy and Doven, and sometimes we didn't. Today we didn't. I wasn't sure if she'd picked up everything that had gone on yesterday and last night, but with the others around, it wasn't the time to ask her. She was dreamy-looking and serene as always, as her white-blonde hair floated around her head. If there was a problem, Ciarissa wasn't allowing it to affect her mood.

"Crew, prepare for jump," Roy said over the intercom.

It's great to say "prepare," but no matter how many times we did it, the jumps to hyperspace were always tough.

The first few moments of a jump made you feel compressed, and all you could see was inky blackness, whether you were looking out a window or not. If Roy or Doven calibrated even a bit incorrectly this would be the last thing any of us would experience and we'd die in suffocating darkness.

Just when you thought you couldn't take the feeling of suspended death any longer, your stomach turned inside out and back again. This fun feeling proved the jump was successful.

All windows, including that of the cockpit, were blacked out to prevent anyone from being able to see what we were flying past. It was great to say "no peeking" but, species nature being what it was, it was much harder to enforce.

Because of the ship's rate of speed as it went into hyperspace, if anyone watched the star systems and gods alone knew what else go past, they'd either go blind or crazy. Someone in the past who'd possessed both technological know-how and a goodly helping of common sense had created a simple sensor that automatically blacked out all viewing portals once a spaceship jumped to hyperspace.

The rest of the flight was fairly nondescript. If I really concentrated I could feel a little extra compression—nothing like the initial jump, more like I was carrying an extra ten pounds on top of my skin.

There were a few species in the galaxy that were so delicate that they could never travel via hyperspace because of this pressure. Taking the sick or injured into hyperspace was also iffy—most of the time it wasn't an issue, but because illness and injury made a being more sensitive, hyperspace could sometimes cause additional health problems.

Most of us shrugged it off and ignored it because the downsides of hyperspace were far outweighed by the advantages of being able to travel all over the galaxy without the trip taking entire lifetimes.

As with our sleep times, Roy insisted on either himself or Doven remaining at the controls. Today they both stayed in the cockpit. I decided not to wander up to see what was going on—hopefully things were fine

and they were making up with each other. If they were fighting, we'd hear it sooner or later.

Instead, I headed for the engine room to see what Willy was up to. Willy was the only true Earther on board — Roy and Kyle were Martian, and so right up there on the popularity rolls with shape shifters and Quillian Shamans. Willy was also the eldest member of the crew — presuming Dr. Wufren was telling the truth, which was never a safe bet.

Willy had done a lot and seen a lot. He'd traveled from one side of the galaxy to the other more times than the rest of us put together. He was our ship's engineer and chief mechanic, though Bullfrog could also cover if needed, and Kyle was learning how to do these jobs as well.

I was unsurprised, therefore, to find Kyle with Willy in the *Hummingbird's* belly.

"Hey, DeeDee, what're you doing here?" Kyle asked from under what might have been a carbine, might have been a drive shaft, or might have been something else entirely. I didn't shift into inanimate objects, so I'd never given the ship's mechanics much attention. That's what Willy, Bullfrog, and, apparently, Kyle were for.

"I can't visit the engine room?"

He was lying on a rolling board that allowed him to slide under engine parts without having to crawl. Willy said the idea came from Old Earth, in the ancient days before space flight. Willy liked using something that had been used by mechanics for millennia.

Kyle rolled closer to me, though he remained on his back. He was a mini-Roy — smaller all the way around, but no one could ever mistake them for anything other than siblings, even with grease over half of Kyle's face. "You almost never come down here," he pointed out. "So, why're you here now? Not that it's not great to see you. My big bro being a pain?"

"No, he's busy and I'm just sort of bored."

"You mean you don't want to find out if Roy and Doven are still fighting."

"You're so much smarter than Roy thinks you are. I'm impressed."

Willy peered over the whatever-it-was they were working on. "Yeah? Then why's the kid covered with grease?"

"Because he idolizes you."

Willy laughed. "You're so good with the flattery, little girl."

"Only when it's deserved." Roy had a great crew, and Willy absolutely belonged with the rest of us. To date, he'd never come across anything mechanical he couldn't figure out, fix, and improve.

Willy walked around to me, wiping his hands on a rag. He was one of those lean men who got a little more sunken and a lot more wiry with age. His hair was still mostly black, though there was, as he put it, a little bit of snow on the mountaintop. "Sure, sure. Kyle, go fetch the magnosensor repair kit. The one I have stored under my bunk."

Kyle scrambled to his feet. "You sure? I thought we had it all fixed."

"You know there's no such thing as thinking out in space, kiddo. You have to be dead sure, or you just wind up dead."

"Yeah, yeah. I know, I know. And I'm going," he added as Willy flicked his rag at Kyle, who trotted off with a laugh.

I waited until I knew Kyle was out of earshot. "So, what's going on?"

Willy grinned. "Can never fool you, can I? I don't know if this is such a good idea."

"Having Kyle get the magnosensor repair kit?"

"Don't play cute with me. You know what I mean."

"Maybe. Going to Polliworld or seeing what's going on with Monte the Leech?"

"Both."

"You love gambling. Actually, I might be understating it—you adore gambling."

"Not more than life itself, little girl."

"We've dealt with Monte for years, I doubt he's going to give us too much trouble."

Willy snorted. "Little girl, if he's made this deal, Monte's already *in* trouble. And Roy's heading us right into the thick of whatever that trouble is. The last place we want to be is caught between the Diamante Families and the Polliworld Underground."

"Okay, I'll give you that would be the proverbial rock and a hard place situation." I considered this. "Do you think Roy knows something?"

"No, I don't. The news caught him as unawares as the rest of us. No, I think Roy's heading us to Polliworld to distract everyone from the fight he's having with Doven—especially himself and Doven."

"Could be. Should I talk to Ciarissa?"

"Nah. No point. Either she's interested or she's not. Besides, that's not the problem. The problem is that

Doven and Roy are having a fundamental disagreement."

"Doven told me he thought Roy was working Ciarissa too hard and that he didn't like anything Roy was asking her to do. I know I was gone for three months, but nothing I've seen since I've been back would make me think Ciarissa's at the point of collapse."

"Right. I don't think that's the real reason they're fighting."

"Why would Doven lie to me?"

"Oh, I'm sure he was telling you the truth. He's been sweet on Ciarissa for as long as she's been with us. But I think there's more to it."

"Any guess as to what? Because I don't have any idea."

"No idea either." Willy cocked his head at me. "But you're the one most likely to get the truth out of Roy. And I suggest you do so, before we all end up caught in the middle of whatever's really going on."

Kyle returned and I wandered off. It didn't take Ciarissa's telepathy to know Willy didn't want to continue our discussion with Roy's little brother present.

I headed for the galley, in part because I was a little hungry and in part because I wanted to get some other opinions. Tresia and Bullfrog were both there—her cooking, him eating—which meant I could get fed and get information at the same time.

"Snack time, DeeDee?" Tresia asked cheerfully. She was busy prepping our next meal, arms going every which way, pincers snapping, stirring, or grabbing depending. Since Arachnidans had eight limbs, this wasn't as hard as it sounded—until you realized she wasn't looking at anything other than me.

"I could be convinced."

Bullfrog grunted as I sat down across from him. "I have some fly pie left."

"Hilarious. I haven't gagged at that one for a long time. Trying out the oldies but goodies to prep for a home world visit?"

Bullfrog shook his head. "I'm hoping to stay on the ship."

"Seriously?"

"Very."

"Why? You were the one who brought the whole thing up."

He grunted. "Yeah. I'm an idiot."

Tresia put a plate of sautéed sandworms in front of me. I hadn't gagged at these for a long time, either. Despite the name, and unlike fly pie, Quillian Sandworms were succulent and delicious, and the way Tresia prepared them made them even better. The sandworms were plump, perfectly browned—crisp on the outside, tender on the inside—with a buttery finish and a hint of cinnamon.

"Yum." Information could wait. I dug in.

"Bullfrog's worried about his cover," Tresia said as I tried not to slurp or shovel the entire plate into my mouth at once. I really loved sautéed sandworms.

"Oh, why?" I asked with my mouth full.

Bullfrog heaved a sigh. "I'm worried that things have...gotten around."

"What things? Tresia, are there any more sandworms?"

She piled more onto my plate. "We have plenty. I stocked up."

"Things like my cover," Bullfrog said as he finished his fly pie. "It's one thing to say I'm part of the Polliworld Underground when we're not there."

"It's never bothered you before. We've gone to Polliworld a lot and this is the first time you've mentioned this worry."

"Yeah, but we've never visited when someone who thinks I'm part of the Polliworld Underground has taken up residence there."

I froze, mid-slurp. "Oh. Would Monte say anything, do you think?"

"I think the Leech would do or say whatever he had to in order to protect himself or give himself an edge. I know he likes us, but I wouldn't trust him as far as you could throw him."

"Since I don't want to touch him, that wouldn't be far."

"Exactly. And I really wish this had occurred to me before I opened my mouth and told Roy what was going on."

Tresia slid a few more sandworms onto my plate. "That's it for you or you won't want any dinner."

"The way everyone's acting, I think I want more, in case it's my last meal."

Bullfrog shook his head. "No joke. If the Underground finds out I've been pretending to work for them, we're going to be in big trouble."

The Polliworld Underground wasn't as bad as the Diamante Families were. No one was. But Polliwogs were exceptionally strong for their size, territorial, and tended toward taciturnity. This hid the fact that they were a lot smarter on average than anyone would think a walking toad could be. The fact that the Underground survived and thrived after the Diamante Purge said a lot about their own cunning—and brutality.

We'd managed to stay pretty clear of any Underground entanglements. So far. But Bullfrog had a good point—if we were about to visit Monte, then we were asking for Underground interaction.

"Do you think Roy's considered this?"

Bullfrog grimaced, an interesting sight on a Polliwog. Somehow, it made his mouth look even larger than it was, which was saying a lot. "I mentioned it to him. He said I was worried for nothing and should take a nap."

I finished my last sandworm and put my plate into the sink. "Yesterday at this time nothing was wrong. I get one good nap in and somehow everything's all messed up."

"That'll teach you to sleep on the job." Bullfrog stood up. "Back to work for me. Maybe if you take another nap everything will go back to normal."

"It never works that way," Tresia said.

"Let's pretend it does. I don't want to give up naps forever." Though I didn't think a nap was a good idea right now. Snooping, not sleeping, was my plan.

"We're coming out of the jump," Roy said over the intercom. "Everyone strap in."

"So much for that," Bullfrog said as he sat back down, pretty much speaking for both of us. Tresia and I joined him as Kyle and Willy confirmed that they were staying in Engineering and were already strapped in. Ciarissa wasn't with us. I didn't know if that meant she was with Roy and Doven or elsewhere, but she didn't check in.

The jump ending wiped thoughts of anything but my stomach out of my mind. I didn't want to revisit my sandworms.

Coming out of hyperspace was always easier than going into it, though your stomach flipping was a given. It just didn't flip as badly.

"Okay, we're at the edge of the Pollisystem," Roy said over the intercom. "Should reach Polliworld in an hour or so. Let's get prepped."

Despite the average being's desire to breathe without snorting down a throat full of flies, Polliworld ran a brisk business in scientific exploration and experimentation. Some came to prove that every world had started like Polliworld, as primordial swamps. Others came to disprove the same theory. There were always some cross-species proponents or opponents around, trying to prove or disprove that the Polliwogs were related to amphibians on other planets.

All of these were outnumbered by the geologists, oceanographers, herpetologists, entomologists, and their ilk who swarmed over Polliworld at all times. Basically, the planet was a scientific playground, and because those scientists were around, Polliworld was almost as popular a destination as Roulette.

Most of the science teams didn't stay long, but they made up for short stays by coming back frequently. And when they went home, the various scientists talked about Polliworld, if only to explain why they'd spent so much money to learn whatever they had, and why they wanted more money to go back and learn even more.

All this somehow translated into the denizens of their particular planets wanting to see Polliworld up close and personally, if only to see if it was really as awful as it appeared to be. Unless you lived for flies, it was, at least if you were outdoors.

Polliworld was a swamp planet. Everything on it had that kind of damp that never goes away. Mold, mildew, and mud were everywhere, and Polliwogs liked it that way. They felt it kept their planet lush and lovely. It also ensured other races weren't going to try to move in and take over. Swamp living was hard on beings who didn't have water-repellent skin and the ability to close their nostrils and still breathe.

The air was technically breathable for all of us, but it was thick with flies and all available surfaces were covered with things that attracted flies and helped them to make more flies. The smell was exactly what you'd expect for a huge, active swamp that doubled as a fly-making factory—fetid. The air quality redefined the term "humid."

The few areas with solid ground went for a premium price—most Polliwogs lived in raised communities, called Pads, which hovered over their particular part of whichever section of swamp their family had claimed generations ago, supported by strong, water-resistant stakes and specialized grav-generators that ran on water power.

Prepping for landing wasn't that big a deal. Polliworld was an older planet and possessed an excellent spaceport that was run efficiently. The risk of crashing existed, of course, but due to the swampy nature of the planet, the risks of injury from a crash landing were minimized.

Well, if we didn't have a Quillian Shaman with us, landing would have been a big deal because we rarely liked to identify who we all really were and most planetary systems liked to know who was dropping by for a visit. Having Doven on the crew meant we could land on most of the planets we visited regularly without worry. Because of this, most of landing prep was on him and Roy.

Doven changed the ship's identifying call numbers on the outer hull of the *Hummingbird* while he also altered a few exterior characteristics of the structure, which changed it into a different ship as far as anyone else would know.

Per Roy's rules, once the call letters were changed, we all stopped calling or thinking of the ship by its real name. For the rest of our time in the Polliworld system we were members of the crew of the *Stingray*.

As far as anyone at Polliworld Mission Control was concerned, the *Stingray* hailed from Oceana and was a science ship, meaning it was a great cover for this world.

So while prepping for landing wasn't that big a deal, prepping for exiting the ship and actually going onto Polliworld was quite a big deal.

"Bullfrog to the cockpit. Everyone not from Polliworld to the hold," Roy said over the intercom.

"Enjoy," Bullfrog said as he left us.

For Bullfrog, the flies in the air meant nothing other than that he could snack any time he wanted simply by putting his tongue out. For the rest of us, it meant wearing the Polliworld equivalent of a space suit, complete with helmet. The suits were the only things that ensured you wouldn't be eaten alive by flies, suffocate from the smell or flies in your nose and mouth, or melt due to the humidity.

"Oh, how I've missed the suit," Tresia said under her breath as she quickly cleaned up the galley. I couldn't blame her for being underwhelmed— Polliskins were hard enough to get into with only four limbs. Eight arms and legs along with an Arachnid body made getting a Polliskin on a galaxy-class sporting event for Tresia and those helping her.

Because we had a Polliwog on crew and visited this world with a certain amount of frequency, we all had our own Polliskins. Doven and Tresia always needed assistance. Sometimes the rest of us did, too. So we'd learned long ago that we all had to get into the suits together.

The experience was always interesting. Usually fun, sometimes fractious, but ultimately bonding.

Once Bullfrog was in the pilot's seat, Roy joined the rest of us in the portion of the hold where we stored our dangerous elements gear.

"Time to get ready for top world diving," Willy said as everyone started to struggle into their Polliskins.

"You say that every time," Kyle said as he helped Doven get his wings into their covering.

"One day we'll go sea diving and you'll have to wear a wetsuit," Willy said with a grin. "They're the only things worse to get into than Polliskins."

"So you've always claimed," I said. "But I don't know how that can be true."

"You're the only one besides Bullfrog who could avoid using the suit," Kyle pointed out.

This was true. I could shape shift into a Polliwog and go in without issue. However, I didn't shift if it wasn't necessary. Polliskins adapted to the person wearing them, so going in with my Polliskin on meant if I had to shift into something other than a Polliwog, I'd still be protected.

Besides, I didn't want to eat flies, and if I shifted into a Polliwog and went outside, I'd have to or I'd stand out as a fake immediately. I'd eaten flies before and probably would again, but there was no reason to do so before it became absolutely necessary.

"She could," Roy said. "But there's no reason for her to be anything other than my cute little redhead right now."

Everyone started teasing Roy, even Doven. It felt like things were back to normal. I hoped this was so, because after talking to Willy and Bullfrog, I had a bad feeling about this particular trip.

As usual, Roy's landing was perfect. The discussion with Bullfrog wasn't customary, however.

"I want to stay on the ship," Bullfrog said for the third time.

"Monte will expect to see you," Roy replied. "It's going to raise more questions for him if you don't show than if you do."

"I'll monitor as well," Ciarissa said.

"If you can," Bullfrog countered. "Just because it's a new casino on a world that doesn't normally require Espens to identify, that doesn't mean Monte won't have installed the usual tele-surveillance."

Shocking absolutely no one, casinos and similar weren't excited to have beings with telepathic and telekinetic powers hanging around. Espens were required to wear complicated head and body gear whenever they left their ships on Roulette and before going into casinos on other planets with gaming establishments, and on some planets without gaming but with a high privacy factor.

Tele-inhibitors had never been required on Polliworld. The Underground wasn't concerned about Espen powers, for whatever reason. However, Bullfrog's point was well made, because Polliworld had also never had a casino before.

Ciarissa closed her eyes and leaned her head back. "I sense no problems, at least within the spaceport. I'll be able to test when we're closer to our destination."

I checked Doven's reaction. Feathers weren't ruffled –Polliskins being what they were, I could still see his feathers and all other features – but I could tell he knew I was watching him, so that didn't mean anything.

"We need to have someone guarding the ship," Bullfrog said, trying a new tactic. "And in this case, I'm the best option."

"Monte will ask questions you don't want us to answer if you're not with us," Roy said patiently.

"Yeah? Well I'll bet he asks some questions we don't want to answer if I *am* along. Starting with 'do you know my friends here?' and ending with 'so you've been lying to me all this time?' I think our best course is me staying on the *Stingray*."

"We have her locked down. I'm the captain, and you're coming along. This is a social call. We're not doing a job—we're visiting a friend."

"Job or not, this is a bad idea, Roy." Bullfrog shook his head, but he stopped arguing. And on that cheerful note, we locked down the *Stingray* and headed for the Spillway.

Polliworld's Tourism Bureau, which was unofficially run by the Underground, had two distinct branches: Scientific and Respite. For first-timers it was easier to get through the Spillway, which was their version of customs, if you were coming through via the Respite side.

However, we'd been here often enough that the *Stingray's* crew and mission were reasonably well-known, and scientific missions were rarely searched because their equipment tended to be fragile and expensive to replace. On Polliworld, whoever broke it bought it, and that rule extended to Polliworld Underground employees. As Bullfrog liked to say, Polliworld Underground was firm but fair.

We arrived to a short line and were up at the head of it in no time. "Business on Polliworld?" the Polliwog working our line asked.

"Crew of the science vessel *Stingray*," Roy said. "Here to continue our research on the habits and lifecycles of leeches."

Ironically, this really was our mission. We'd created it in honor of Monte, but without his knowledge, of course.

"Where's your equipment?" the clerk asked.

"On our ship," Roy replied. "We want to determine where we'll be studying before we haul it all out."

"And we want to see your new gaming establishment," Ciarissa added with a beaming smile.

The Polliwog nodded. "Good. We're very proud of it."

"We heard about it from six solar systems away," Dr. Wufren said. "Made us get ready in a hurry."

The Polliwog smiled. "Length of stay?"

"Unsure," Roy said. "Let's request the maximum, if we may, just to be on the safe side."

"One Polliworld month," our clerk said as he stamped nine bright green leaflets and handed them to Roy. They really were leaves, from one of the sturdier and abundant trees that grew on Polliworld like weeds. Polliwogs preferred to use natural products whenever possible.

Roy handed us each one. They were stamped for a month's stay with full access. I wondered if Ciarissa had helped the Polliwog to be amenable or if we'd just caught him on a good day. Normally we had to work a little harder to get this kind of all access pass.

Once you'd landed at a spaceport and made it past the Spillway, Polliworld was fairly lax about everything else. The Underground tended to protect itself, and therefore its planet, quite well. The positive of being thought of as scientists here was easy and reasonably unhindered access. The negative was that all our weapons were still on the *Stingray*. It was an unpleasant but necessary tradeoff.

We left the Spillway area, unmolested and basically ignored. It was a nice feeling – experience said this level of casual disinterest wouldn't last.

"Ready to get to work?" Roy asked me.

"Sure. Let's head off to study the habits of Monte the Leech and to determine if his lifecycle is in danger."

Monte had taken up residence in Amphibia, the capitol city of Polliworld. The Amphibia Space Center was huge and had anything and everything you could want: a museum, a theme park, the Swampland Zoo, restaurants, gift shops, and more. Anything made on or about Polliworld—including Polliskins and various transportation methods—were for sale or rent. Some visitors to Polliworld never left the Space Center and still felt they'd really seen the planet.

Enclosed buildings were fly-, humidity-, and fetid-odors-free. I could see the wisdom in never leaving the Space Center.

I was somewhat surprised Monte's establishment wasn't attached to the Space Center. I had no clue whether this was a sound idea or not, or if the casino was elsewhere because the Underground wanted Monte elsewhere. Either way, I planned to find out.

"Can you tell if it's safe?" Roy asked Ciarissa.

"Especially for you and Dr. Wufren," Doven added.

"Not yet. We're too far away." Ciarissa could read minds from space if necessary, but spotting electronic and mechanical surveillance and related equipment required closer proximity. Dr. Wufren was telekinetic, not telepathic, so he normally needed Ciarissa to know what items might need to be moved, shut down, tampered with, or broken—and when.

"We'll go along and if we have to take public transportation to return to the safety of the Space Center, we will," Dr. Wufren said. "Don't worry, my boys, we can take care of ourselves."

"The Underground taking care of all of us is what worries me," Bullfrog muttered under his breath. If Roy heard him, he ignored Bullfrog's fretting.

We rented a planet flyer and headed for The Polliwog Palace. Monte was all about keeping the theme if the original had worked out well.

Amphibia, like the other Polliworld cities, was on dry ground. But the swamp-and-flies motif was in full force anyway, making visibility sketchy. All this caused a first-time visitor to assume that Polliworld ground transportation went slowly and carefully and was well-controlled at all times.

Which is why so many first-time visitors ended up in the hospital.

Polliwogs made good pilots in space, and even in the air, but they were awful flyers on the ground for whatever reason. Maybe it was because the more flies they could smash onto their windshields meant the bigger, better meal later, but "chaotic" was the kindest description I could ever come up with for how they flew.

"They all drive like little old ladies with a death wish," Willy said as Roy dodged the first, but certainly not the last, near crash. "It's like they can't see and have the accelerator pressed down to the floorboards."

He was right and I was glad Roy was driving— even Doven would have had difficulty avoiding the planet flyers going every which way at reckless speeds with no obvious directional goals in mind.

"You say that every time," Kyle mentioned through clenched teeth.

"It's true every time," Willy replied with a hiss as a flyer missed us by a hair's breadth. "This place is like running a gauntlet—bad all the way through with death likely waiting for you at the end."

"Cut the chatter," Bullfrog said. "Roy needs to concentrate."

This was true and we all shut up, other than group and individual gasps of fear as we ran the traffic gauntlet and prayed to our personal gods for safe passage.

Proving again that he was the best at any kind of piloting, Roy got us to the Polliworld Palace unscathed. He went to self-parking, and no one argued. The walk was longer, but you didn't have to wait for someone to bring your flyer around if a fast retreat was necessary. And fast retreat was frequently necessary for us.

"What do you get here?" Roy asked Ciarissa.

She closed her eyes and tilted her head back again. "Nothing. There is no telepathic surveillance or telekinetic inhibition I can detect."

"That's odd," Willy said.

"Scary," Bullfrog suggested.

"Good for us," Dr. Wufren offered.

"I'm with the doctor," Roy said. "Let's go. But everyone be ready for anything."

"You know," Kyle said. "Business as usual."

The downside of using general parking was that it wasn't enclosed. Thankfully, we had our Polliskins. However, we were either going to have to keep them on inside or leave them at the spacesuit check, which was never a good plan for us.

Bullfrog's unease convinced Roy to have us keep our Polliskins on. However, as we entered the antechamber that connected self-parking with the casino's lobby and took a look around, everyone who had a 'Skin was checking it.

Bullfrog was looking elsewhere. "Is there really no tele-surveillance of any kind around?" he asked in a low voice.

"I sense none," Ciarissa reassured him.

"Nor I," Dr. Wufren said. "Nothing seems to be inhibiting me in any way."

Roy looked at Ciarissa. She nodded. *"We will do as the others,"* she said in our heads.

We waited for a contingent of Polliwogs with bad attitudes to descend on us, but nothing happened.

We heaved a collective sigh and struggled out of the 'Skins. Dr. Wufren used his powers to help Doven and Tresia out of their 'Skins. No one took any kind of interest in us.

"Don't get cocky," Bullfrog warned. "Just because you can't spot it and no one's come to slap you two into tele-restraints doesn't mean they're not monitoring."

"Bullfrog's right," Roy said. "Only use your talents for what's necessary for the job, not for anything else."

Dr. Wufren sighed. "You do like to remove all the fun out of life sometimes, my boy." He grinned as Roy and Bullfrog glared at him. "Not to worry. We'll be the souls of discretion."

The Polliwogs working in coat check were younger females. Kyle and Bullfrog checked our suits in—Kyle flirted, Bullfrog blew his cheeks out, the females giggled and promised to keep our gear very safe. Two of them passed their cards to Bullfrog. One passed hers to Kyle. "I like off-worlders," she said, loud enough for the rest of us to hear.

Kyle grinned, Bullfrog looked pleased with himself, and Roy blushed. Roy's extremely old-fashioned reactions toward the variety of come-ons he, and to an extent Kyle, always got was always endearing.

"Nice to see your charm is still working," I said to Bullfrog as we walked along the enclosed corridor.

"I'm the best there is at cheek puffing."

"That's what it says on the bathroom stalls," Willy said.

I managed to refrain from comment, or laughter, but only because I'd known Bullfrog a long time. Every species had their own special mating rituals.

The reminder that I no longer had the option to practice the rituals specific to my species slithered up from the part of my mind where I'd shoved those regrets. I had Roy, and really, I didn't need someone who could shape shift to make me happy. Even if I met another shifter—an unlikely possibility since the Diamante Purge—I'd want him to shift into a copy of Roy anyway.

I enjoyed that particular sexual fantasy, because the idea of having two Roys making love to me was only supplanted by the idea of having three.

"What are you smirking about?" Kyle asked me.

I quickly shoved regrets about the loss of my entire race and sexual fantasies about his big brother out of my mind, but not before Ciarissa giggled. I figured my fantasy had been particularly "loud" in my mind and did my best not to blush. "Nothing, nothing. Where the heck is Monte's office in this place, do you think?"

"No idea," Roy said with a shrug.

Ciarissa's eyes narrowed. "We must go through the casino, I believe."

"Never a problem, my dear," Dr. Wufren said cheerfully as he offered his arm to Ciarissa, and they led the way. The rest of us followed.

The Palace on Roulette was large, loud, and flashy. Monte had done his level best to ensure the Polliworld Palace was larger, louder and, galaxy gods alone knew how, flashier.

Everyone inside seemed to be having a fabulous time. The noise level was high, with a lot of whooping and excited squealing. There weren't just Polliwogs in here, either—a variety of beings from other systems had come by to check out the new game in town. The Polliwog Palace was packed.

Normally I enjoyed the flashiness that casinos created—it was fun to be around and the glitz, and constant activity made it easier to shift without being spotted.

However, shape shifters were, among our other talents, really good at spotting fakes. We had to be, in order to learn and protect ourselves. I took another good look around. Under the circumstances, it felt like everyone was trying just a little too hard.

Dr. Wufren and Ciarissa led us on a winding path through the casino. We looked like we were just wandering, which was wiser than heading directly for the heart of the operation. Beings who appeared to be storming the place where the surveillance feeds and money were housed tended to be removed bodily.

We finally reached a hallway at the back of the casino, set off from the main floor in such a way that it was easy to miss unless you were looking for it or, in the case of our group, had a telepath along.

We trotted down the corridor until we reached a doorway at the end of the hall. A doorway with guards. Big Polliwogs who made Bullfrog look puny. Clearly, we'd arrived.

Roy stepped to the front. "Here to see Monte the Leech," he said to the two huge, stone-faced guards. Of course, Polliwogs looked stone-faced frequently, but it was clear these two practiced in the mirror every morning.

"Who wants to see Mister Leech?" one of the guards asked.

"Roy."

"Roy who?" the other guard asked. They both seemed willing to wait a long time for the answer.

"Doctor Roy Evans." Roy wasn't a doctor and Evans certainly wasn't his last name, but using his last name would be the height of stupidity here. It would be the same as us waving a banner saying "Look! It's the Last of the Imperius Bloodline!" in front of the entire Diamante hit squad.

"And why would Mister Leech want to see a doctor?" the first guard asked.

"Routine checkup," Roy said, sounding bored. "Here to ensure that Mister Leech's parts don't fall off."

The stone-faces remained stable, but the door opened. "Roy baby, how're they hangin'?" a familiar voice called from inside. "You and the rest of my favorite crazy crew should come on in."

We did as requested. The Polliwogs looked disappointed for a moment and then went back to practicing for their second jobs as statues.

The room was large and lavish, decorated in what I thought of as Bad Guy Impressive. Lots of large, dark, heavy, obviously expensive furniture, thick rugs, a heavy reliance on gilt and deep reds. Monte liked style, even though it was hard for him to achieve it personally.

My gaze landed on Monte, and I managed to hide my involuntary shudder. I'd known Monte a long time, but seeing him was still repulsive, at least at first blush. He wasn't called "the Leech" only because he drained your money.

Monte undulated over. He did some intricate hand slapping with Roy, Kyle, Willy, Bullfrog and, even more impressively, Tresia. I focused on his hands. They hadn't been his originally, but it's amazing what some people had to give up when they lost more money than they actually had access to. And the medical advances on Roulette were legendary. Another reason Monte moving to Polliworld was odd.

Doven and Monte did a wing-butt thing that never failed to make me want to gag. For whatever reason, Monte didn't ever try to touch Dr. Wufren or Ciarissa. Lucky them.

Monte looked at me. "What, no hug for your Uncle Monte?" He looked expectant, at least as much as a giant leech with hands and other, thankfully covered, parts could.

I sighed to myself. I knew the drill. If I didn't come across, we didn't get our money, information, or cut of the action. Monte was a traditionalist, when you got right down to it. And while he was untrustworthy in many things, he was one of the few beings I knew wouldn't turn me in as a shifter any more than he'd turn Roy and Kyle in as the last of the Imperious line. As long as I humored him.

I shifted and was now a female giant leech, also with hands, but no other parts Monte could conceivably feel. I undulated to him, and we sort of lolled into each other.

Most disgusting species greeting in the galaxy over, I shifted back to me, and Monte beamed. "Lord of the flies, it's been too long. What brings you out my way? Can't wait to test your luck on my lovely new tables?" He directed this remark specifically to Willy and Dr. Wufren.

"No." Roy shot the two of them a very meaningful glance that plainly said "behave." He looked back to Monte. "No, we wanted to know what's going on."

"New scenery's good for the soul, Roy baby."

"Right." Roy looked around. "This place bugged?"

"Of course not!" Monte said with just a little too much enthusiasm. "I've got free rein here. Best setup in the galaxy."

"Fren has disconnected the audio and visual surveillance," Ciarissa shared. "I believe we will have a few minutes before company arrives."

"Fine," Roy said, more to Ciarissa and Dr. Wufren than to Monte. "So, for the short time we'll be able to visit with you, why don't you tell us why you sold part interest in the Palace to the Diamante Families?"

"Business, Roy baby. Business. They made me an offer I couldn't refuse."

"What were they going to do to you if you did refuse?" I asked.

Monte shrugged, which meant his whole body rippled. I managed not to gag again, but only barely. "They're business-beings, I'm a business-being. It's not like I'm in bed with Roman the Redeemer or something."

The Redeemer had been one of the political leaders on Convent—a religious, peaceful planet. Until the Diamante Purge, anyway. Roman had given up on peace and fought back, very publicly, and in a variety of dirty ways, ultimately becoming a guerilla fighter with a good sized fleet. By then, he'd become a fanatic and had perpetrated atrocities on more than the Diamante Families—he'd attacked worlds unwillingly under Diamante control. Not to free them, but to do his own kind of purge.

But the Diamante Families were too much for even Roman and his fanatical followers. The Redeemer's fleet was destroyed, and the story went, he'd been run underground.

These days, the Redeemer was used as a boogeyman, someone to mention to show that while you might be bad, you weren't *that* bad.

"If he came by with a deal, you'd think about it," Roy noted. Accurately.

Monte shrugged and rippled again. I again controlled the gag impulse while hoping we'd have no more shrugging from him for a while. I wasn't sure I could continue to keep my sandworms down. "We reached a mutually satisfying arrangement. Which meant I could come here." Monte beamed. "I'm on the ground floor of what's going to be a huge industry."

"Speaking of which, why are you in bed with the Underground?" Roy asked.

"As if you're not?" Monte said, nodding toward Bullfrog.

"Not the same thing," Roy said. "And you know it. Look, Monte, we want in on the action."

Monte's beaming smile faltered. "No can do, Roy baby. No can do."

"Why not? Since when have you ever cut us out?"

I could think of plenty of times, but now wasn't a good moment to bring them up. Roy was mostly correct—when it had mattered, Monte had always cut us in. Not so much because he wanted to support the Martian Alliance—Monte didn't care all that much about restoring the galaxy to its former, and rightful, rulers as some did—but because he was smart enough to want to always stay in good with those currently in power and those who might one day have power again.

Monte sighed. "Since I don't have a choice. I have plenty of partners already. I don't need more." He dropped his voice. "And you don't want in on this, trust me."

"Why not?" Roy asked.

"It's...complicated." Monte pointedly looked at the wall behind us.

I took a look. The wall wasn't exceptional in any way, but there was a rendering of a lot of large, flashy buildings. I stepped closer. "Casino City" was written at the bottom. "Why wouldn't we want in on an entire Polliworld city dedicated to gambling?"

"Look closer," Monte said. "Look very close."

The others joined me and we all stared at the big picture. "Where's Orion's Light?" Kyle asked finally. He pointed to a small legend in the lower corner of the rendering—Casino City looked to be taking up half of an entire globe.

"Ah, good eye!" Monte said heartily. "It's a moon at the outskirts of the Betelgeuse system. It's been colonized by those of an...understanding bent."

"You mean they don't have a lot of laws," Roy translated.

"Exactly, baby, exactly. Perfect place for the next Palace."

"You just opened this one," I pointed out. "Why are you looking to expand again before this place could have possibly turned a profit?"

"DeeDee, you wound your Uncle Monte. We were in the black within the first day's opening."

"I've been all over the galaxy and I've never heard of this particular rock," Willy said, before I could mention that I found it close to impossible to believe that Monte had covered all the startup costs of a huge casino in one month, let alone in a day. The overly happy people on the casino floor said differently as well. Shills cost money, especially shills being asked to do the level of acting those in the casino were putting forth.

"Newly colonized," Monte replied nonchalantly.

"When?" Roy asked. "We keep track of the inhabiteds. And Willy's right—I've never heard of Orion's Light, and it hasn't come up on our schematics or maps."

"The decision to colonize was made quickly," Monte said. "The Betelgeuse system's allowed the pleasure of gambling close to home, just like the Polliworld system."

"Who's invested in Orion's Light?" I asked. "Besides you, I mean."

"You all should take some time and enjoy the gaming," Monte said, more than obviously ignoring my question.

"We should leave, immediately," Ciarissa said in our heads. "We have company coming, and they are equipped to make life very painful for Fren and myself."

"We'll talk more about this later," Roy said.

Monte nodded. "Feel free to leave via the owner's entrance. It's very private." He nodded his head toward a dark corner of the office. I couldn't see any door there, but looking there was better than looking at Monte undulate to the doors we'd used to enter the room.

Ciarissa nodded and Roy headed for the part of the room Monte had indicated. Dr. Wufren put his hand out and a panel opened silently. "Nice work, Mister Leech," he said as he stepped aside to let Bullfrog go through first.

"Thank you, sir," Monte replied. "Don't be strangers."

We hurried through the hidden doorway. Roy and I were last. As the door closed behind us I heard Monte. "Gentlemen! What a lovely surprise."

"Nice to see he's covering for us," I said softly as we followed the others down a very sturdy, very non-flashy corridor.

"If he really is," Roy replied as we reached an intersection.

"To the right takes us outside," Ciarissa said. "To the left returns us to the casino."

"Well, we need to go back to the casino to get our 'Skins," Kyle pointed out.

"A large number of Polliworld Underground personnel are on premises," Ciarissa shared. "They are looking for Fren and myself."

"Because I blocked surveillance, my dear? I did my best to make it look like equipment failure."

Ciarissa shook her head slowly. "You did a good job with that, Fren. No, I believe we tripped another form of surveillance. One none of us spotted."

"We need to know what spotted us," Roy said, "or else we can't counter it next time, let alone as soon as we walk through the door back into the casino."

Ciarissa shook her head. "I don't know. I can pick up nothing untoward."

"Maybe Monte did it," Kyle suggested.

"It's as likely a possibility as any other," I agreed.

"I knew this was a bad idea," Doven said under his breath. There'd been a lot of muttering on this trip, which wasn't really normal for our crew.

"Fine, let's get out of here and worry about who tripped what another time. We need a distraction," Roy said, "that's all."

"What do you propose?" Bullfrog asked. "We walked in here without a plan for getting out, and they've got us on holographic for sure."

"They don't know who we are," Roy said. "We're scientists here on a mission, remember? We even told the Spillway clerk we were going to check out the new casino. We have every right to be here."

"But we don't," Ciarissa said, indicating herself and Dr. Wufren.

Everyone's expressions were stressed and worried. I had no idea why. The solution seemed obvious. I heaved a sigh. "Everyone, just calm down. We need those 'Skins and Ciarissa and our good doctor need to get back to the *Stingray*. So, not to worry—one Underground distraction coming up."

With that, I concentrated and shifted.

"Nice job," Roy said. "Now we have two of Ciarissa. How is that helping?"

"They're looking for something that an Espen triggered, but it's likely that all they have to go on is holographic feeds of the people who went down the corridor to see Monte." I spent the time I was talking modulating my voice to sound as close to Ciarissa's as possible.

I'd shifted into a likeness of her before. I'd ensured I knew how to shift into any one of us, just in case. Modestly speaking, I was the best shifter around, even before the Diamante Purge. It was one of the reasons I was still alive and able to shift.

Internal shifting was as important as external in many cases, and I knew this would be one of them. This was one of the areas I excelled at, but even for the best, there were limits. Ciarissa and Dr. Wufren presented a challenge I had yet to surmount— telepathic brains were distinctly different from non-telepathic, in part because they were in a constant state of subtle flux. So far I'd been unable to come even close to recreating the same inner workings as Dr. Wufren possessed, let alone Ciarissa. But in this situation, that lack was the strength of my plan.

"You want to be arrested?" Roy looked worried and protective. It was sweet, but I was a little worried myself. He wasn't usually this slow on the uptake.

"No. I can't imitate an Espen mind. They're too complex even for someone with my level of shifting skill, you know that."

"So?" Roy got a lot of worry into that one syllable.

Doven chuckled. "They'll spend their time on DeeDee who won't trigger the right things because her mind isn't actually capable of any form of tele-talent, and the rest of us will get our 'Skins and get out of here. Good plan."

"Terrible plan," Roy snapped. "Espens look like regular humanoids. If they can figure out that Ciarissa and Doctor Wufren are tele-capable without our being able to spot their tele-surveillance that means they have equipment we're not familiar with. And that equipment might show them what DeeDee really is."

"Do you have a better idea with a higher chance of success?"

Roy's expression told me he didn't. I squeezed his hand. "I'll be fine. Just get into those 'Skins, take mine with you, and get the flyer ready and waiting for me. I have no idea which exit I'll be coming out of, but I think it's a safe bet and even odds that when I leave the building I'll be running."

Bullfrog seemed to be struggling with something. "You can't go alone."

"Why not?"

"Because you're going to need backup, and that backup needs to understand how the Underground works as well as how to get to the Space Center in case the others can't wait. Only one of us can do all that, and that means I'm going with DeeDee."

Roy grimaced. "Fine, you both win on this one. Anyone else going to decide to be a renegade or tell me what we're doing?"

"No," Tresia said, as she snipped part of the lining of her cloak. Pincers were really useful appendages. "However, I believe Ciarissa needs to wear a head covering." She wrapped the lining around Ciarissa's head in the same way that religious adherents from Convent wore their head coverings.

"Sure, since you asked." Kyle grinned. "I think I should be in charge from now on. And I think we need to ensure Bullfrog and I get to take those coat check girls out."

"We need to go in teams to the coat check," Roy said. "Worry about dating later."

"Great idea, Tresia. The rest of you can all fight this out while Bullfrog and I go start our distraction. But hurry it up, and save the real arguments for when we're back on the *Stingray*." With that, I headed off down the corridor that took us back to the casino floor.

Interestingly enough, the door at the end of the corridor wasn't being guarded. Either Monte had covered really well, or he'd sent them after us and the Underground enforcers were actually behind us.

"What's your plan, DeeDee?"

Since Bullfrog had said he was coming with me, I'd been revising my plan to utilize all the options now available.

"We're going to head into the casino, in the opposite direction from the coat check. Either they'll go after us and our distraction will evolve naturally, or I'll pick a suitably big being and bump into them, and you'll act like a drunk, jealous boyfriend."

"I can do that." Bullfrog opened the door carefully. "Huh. No guards."

"Does that mean we're lucky or that this entire thing is some kind of huge trap?"

"No bet."

Bullfrog took my hand, and we sauntered down a short corridor that led to a bank of flashing machines. The people at them were, to a one, having the time of their lives. It still rang as overacting to me, but I'd worry about it when we were somewhere safer than we were right now.

We weaved nonchalantly through this section and back onto the main casino floor. Despite Ciarissa having telepathically spotted people after us, we were still amazingly unmolested.

I took a casual look around. It was easy to do, because of the floating hair. As I moved my head, the hair moved more slowly, so I could look through it without appearing to be able to see.

And what I saw was Kyle, Willie, and Dr. Wufren wandering calmly through the casino. Roy, Ciarissa, Doven, and Tresia were behind them, but not looking like they were together. They filtered through the casino toward the main entrance.

A group of Polliwogs wearing suits were hovering around the main entrance. Polliwogs rarely wore suits, because they were heavy and confining. However, in the Underground, wearing a suit indicated you were a high-level enforcer of some kind.

Another group of suit-wearers came out of the same dark corridor we'd gone down to visit Monte, not the one we'd left through, which was good. They were looking around, which wasn't. Time to put on the show.

We were near a pair of roulette tables. Their wheels were spinning, the balls were dropped, and there was a lot of money on both.

"Going with Plan B," I whispered to Bullfrog. Then I laughed loudly. "You're crazy – I have *not* had 'too much'!" Announcement of my lack of inebriation made so that anyone nearby could hear, I "tripped" and slammed into one of the roulette dealers.

He might be a Polliwog, but he was unprepared for me to body slam him. He lost his balance, falling onto his wheel.

I "bounced" off of him and hit the other dealer back to back. This one had been no more prepared than her co-worker, and she went over, too.

This all happened quickly. Clearly this wasn't in the script, because the shills at the tables all gaped. A couple shrieked.

"Oooh, I'm so sorry," I said. "Did I mess up all the chips?" The dealers were recovering themselves, and the Polliwogs in the suits were taking an interest in us.

"You're drunk," Bullfrog said flatly.

"But there's all that money on the tables," I said plaintively, but loud enough to carry. "I want some."

"We're going home," Bullfrog said sternly. He took my hand and pulled me to him. I "stumbled" and shoved him into several beings behind him, which caused a domino effect. They were knocked over, and they knocked the blackjack table they were at over. There were now chips and money all over the place, and some of the shills realized that chaos meant they could possibly grab some extra money.

I heard a few squeals, and then some of the Arachnidans started using those extra limbs to grab money. Seeing this, the others at the tables decided not to miss out. The dealers tried to protect the chips and money, and the scramble started. It went chaotic quickly, which was my goal.

Bullfrog and I extracted ourselves from the growing mob as the Polliwogs in suits decided that whatever was going on in our section was more important than finding the tele-talented. They were joined in this by a goodly contingent of Polliwogs working security.

"We have our Polliskins," Ciarissa said in our heads. "The people looking for Fren and myself have all been distracted by the two of you."

"Time to run," Bullfrog said quietly. He took my hand again, and we headed for what a tiny sign proclaimed to be the rear exit.

We reached the exit door just ahead of the Polliwogs after us. The door was made of tinted glass, so you could see who was coming in or who was outside if you were up close. The area outside this door looked clear.

Unfortunately, the door happened to be locked.

Conveniently, the first Polliwog to reach us grabbed Bullfrog and threw him against the glass door.

"We don't like your kind in here," the Polliwog shared.

Bullfrog was big and the glass wasn't strong enough to withstand a big Polliwog body being flung against it. The glass cracked. "What kind? I'm from here, just like you," Bullfrog said as he kicked the guy who'd grabbed him in the gut.

Several of the suits jumped on Bullfrog. He was good, and kept most of them occupied enough that he didn't go down.

"Stay out of our business, Diamante scum," another Polliwog snarled as he reached for me. I dodged. Now

wasn't the time to question who they thought we were working for. Now was the time to get away.

Ciarissa wasn't the strongest being in the galaxy. However, the benefits of being a shifter were many times without number, and this was one of those times. I kept my external self the same, but altered my insides to match the strength and internal structure of the Troglodytes from Rockenroll, who were similar to the trolls of ancient fairy tales. They lived in caves. Lavish and elaborate caves, but caves nonetheless.

They were also hella strong.

I grabbed the nearest Polliwog in a suit and slammed him into the breaking glass door as hard as I could. I was quite small for a Troglodyte, but even though I was the height of a little child on Rockenroll, I had more than enough strength to use the Polliwog as a battering ram.

The door shattered. I kicked the various suits away from Bullfrog, grabbed him, and ran. Troglodytes weren't fast. All that heavy body with bones and muscles the consistency of rock meant moving fast wasn't in their game plan. However, it was in mine.

I shifted internally again, this time I took on the characteristics of the Naynek from Paradise. As with the Troglodytes, my size meant I was at the level of a child in terms of Naynek abilities, but since they were among the fastest runners in the galaxy, even their young moved swiftly.

This helped us to get away from the casino, but without a Polliskin, I wasn't going to be able to keep up my pace too long.

Bullfrog knew. He lifted me up and flipped me onto his back. "Hold on." Then he took off in the manner all

Polliwogs can, but which he rarely did—he jumped. Bullfrog kicked off with his strong back legs, and we soared into the air. He landed on all fours, his hands helping to keep us balanced. Then he jumped over and over again. He covered a lot of ground this way.

The Underground chased us for a while, but suits aren't well equipped for the kind of leaping Bullfrog was doing, so we lost them. Or they gave up. Or both. I chose not to worry about whether we'd outpaced them or they'd gotten tired of running after us. I was too busy trying not to scream or breathe.

I thought Bullfrog would stop leaping once we lost the Underground, but he didn't. He headed instead for what I knew was the poorer district of Amphibia. After a few minutes, Bullfrog leaped us into some thick, tall reeds that provided an illusion of privacy for those Polliwogs who needed to relieve themselves and couldn't make it to, or be bothered to find, an actual bathroom.

"You need to change into a Polliwog," he said urgently. "Now."

"Gladly." I shifted and was now a female Polliwog. Sure, I was a female Polliwog covered with the remains of what seemed like a million flies on me, but as a Polliwog, it didn't bother me as much as it could have. Which is to say I could wait to throw up until we were back on the *Stingray*.

"Follow me," Bullfrog said, as he leaped away.

I did as requested. As a Polliwog, I enjoyed that the air didn't really feel uncomfortable, the scent of fetid rot was quite pleasing, and the abundance of flies made my stomach rumble. Okay, I enjoyed two out of those three.

We jumped for a good fifteen minutes, and then Bullfrog seemed to feel we were far enough away from danger that we could slow down. Or he was lost. I voted for lost.

We were in a vast, unsettled area of swamp with no Pads anywhere, or dry land. The area had no scientific teams visible. It was, for Polliworld, quite desolate — meaning there were only about a million snakes and a quadrillion bugs along with the zillion flies enjoying the massive and plentiful foliage.

"Where are we?"

Bullfrog sighed. "The only place we're safe right now."

"And where is that?"

The look on Bullfrog's face said that I wasn't going to like the answer. "Probably the most dangerous spot on Polliworld. What we call No Frog's Land."

"Why is it you know about this place?" Good, good. I was calm. At least I sounded calm. I resisted the desire to eat some flies to calm my supposedly calm nerves. Hey, I freely admit to being a stress eater.

Bullfrog grimaced. "This is where I'm from — where I grew up."

I looked around. "Really? Because, I don't see a lot of 'from' around here."

"Trust me."

"Doing my best. Why do you think the Underground called us Diamante scum? We don't look like Diamante employees, let alone enforcers."

"My bet? Monte told them about me and they think I'm a Diamante spy."

The temptation to say that I doubted we were that lucky was strong, but I held it in. "Can Roy and the others come get us here?"

Bullfrog shook his head. "We need to get underground."

"I thought we wanted to avoid the Underground."

He heaved a sigh. "I mean the real underground." Bullfrog took my hand and led me into the swamp.

"Ick. And I mean that in the most species-loving way possible."

"Close your nose and mouth."

"What about my eyes?"

"If you did a full change, you should be fine, but you can close them if you want. I won't lose you."

I ensured I had as good a grip on Bullfrog as he did me. We waded further into the swamp. I did my best to ignore anything and everything I felt brushing against my legs. "Are Polliwogs immune to venomous snake and bug bites?"

"No."

"Fantastic." I took a deep breath and slammed my nose, mouth, and eyes shut as we went under the swamp water.

Bullfrog led me along to somewhere. I refused to look. It was probably stupid, seeing as if I had to run away, or swim really fast, I wouldn't know where to run or swim to. I decided that ignorance was a lot better than the knowledge of exactly what I was swimming next to and through.

We surfaced and I cracked one eyelid. A small patch of dry ground was ahead of us and we clambered onto it. I was never so grateful to feel terra-at-least-sorta-firma in my entire life. "Where are we?" I asked, trying to move my mouth as little as possible, lest I swallow something.

"We're on Longdaddy's Land."

"Longdaddy?"

"He runs No Frog's Land."

"Longdaddy? I mean, I've heard of ensuring you advertise and all that, but, really? Longdaddy?"

A throat cleared behind me. "Yes." The voice was deep and old, but it didn't sound weak in any way.

I turned around slowly to see a very long-legged, very muscular Polliwog of indeterminate advanced age. I could tell he was old because his scales had the whitish tinge only older Polliwogs got.

He held a thick walking stick that I was quite sure doubled as a handy, effective, and painful fighting staff.

"I am Longdaddy," he said, probably for effect, because it wasn't like I couldn't have guessed. "And you are not one of my people."

Self-preservation ensured that I kept my mouth shut even as I tensed to jump. Polliwogs jumped a lot faster and farther than they could run. Not that Bullfrog gave me time to talk, or jump, and he tightened his hold on my hand. "No, she's not from our part of the pond, but she's my friend."

Longdaddy studied us. "A special friend?"

"Very," Bullfrog said firmly.

Every time I went undercover Roy worried that I'd have to make out, or more, with someone other than Roy himself. I always managed to avoid it, but the thought occurred that I might not be able to avoid sharing tongue with Bullfrog, at least if we wanted to survive. This was an unappealing thought on so many levels I lost count.

Longdaddy continued to study us. I wasn't sure if I should attempt to cuddle with Bullfrog, say something, or jump like hell, and Bullfrog wasn't giving me any clues to work with, either.

"What is your 'friend's' name?" Longdaddy asked finally.

"DeeDee," Bullfrog replied.

"I would like her to speak. Especially because DeeDee is not a common name among us."

This was true enough. "It's a nickname," I said which was also true.

"And what is the name you were given when you were a tadpole?" Longdaddy asked me. "I would like you to answer this, not Bullfrog."

"My tad-name is Deciduous. Everyone else always gets called Deci or Dous. I wanted to be different."

Longdaddy seemed thrown, possibly because he hadn't expected me to use a common Polliwog name, let alone know what the standard shortenings of said name were. You didn't survive as long as a hidden shifter as I had without doing a great deal of planetary homework.

"You are Bullfrog's friend?"

"Yes, his very good friend, and he's my very good friend. I don't know that you're our friend, though you may be more friendly than the 'Wogs we just escaped."

Longdaddy's eyes narrowed. "You have angered the Underground?" he asked Bullfrog.

"In a way," Bullfrog replied. "We're…investigating the new casino."

"Ah." Longdaddy appeared to reach a decision. "Come with me. We will discuss your predicament at greater length in better private."

That there were Polliwogs hidden and watching us to protect Longdaddy was a given. I wasn't sure that going into a private meeting with Longdaddy was an improvement.

Bullfrog tugged on my hand, and we followed Longdaddy. He walked off the small patch of land, and we followed into another part of the swamp, with me keeping my Polliwog stone face on and going strong.

We didn't submerge. We walked for quite a ways through swamp, onto small patches of land, back into swamp, and on, wandering in various directions in what felt like a very aimless manner. I had no idea where in the swamp we were, which was, I was sure, the entire point of this particular swampy constitutional.

We finally reached yet another small patch of land, but this one had a reed hut sitting on it. It resembled the standard Polliwog Pads in the same way the *Stingray* resembled a Diamante cruiser—there were similarities, but Longdaddy's hut wasn't giving off the Happy Home kind of aura.

Longdaddy indicated we should precede him inside the hut. I wasn't a fan of this idea, but Bullfrog didn't hesitate. He ducked his head and walked through, dragging me after him.

Sadly, the interior wasn't somehow more huge and palatial inside. It was still a grungy reed hut. However, what it lacked in ambiance it made up for with a stairway going down. Naturally, the stairway was dark, because the cosmos didn't allow it to be any other way.

Longdaddy joined us, then shocked me to my currently-amphibious-core and headed down the stairs in front of us, instead of making us go first into the dark and likely dangerous unknown, stabbing us in the backs, or shoving us down the stairs. Bullfrog heaved a sigh of what was either relief or terror, and headed us down as well.

The walk was long, smelly, and dark. I was glad I was in full Polliwog form, because if it smelled to me in *this* form, I'd have probably passed out from stench overload as my normal self.

We'd gone down a lot of steps, and my eyes adjusted to the dark before we ever reached the end. It was a safe bet that we were underneath the swamp, which meant I needed to focus on the fact that I could swim to the top should the tunnel we were in collapse on us. This was easier said than done.

After what seemed like a good day's worth of walking—but what I was sure was probably only a couple of miles—we hit another stairway and went up and exited into another reed hut, this one no better than the one we'd left earlier, but containing two staircases. We went down the other one, and did the whole fun thing all over again. And then again.

The one thing I was sure of was that we weren't backtracking. I examined the insides of the huts. They were similar but not exact, and I hadn't seen the same one twice.

Five more times and this time when we exited into the latest reed hut, while it had another staircase leading down, we didn't use it. Longdaddy stepped out of the hut.

Bullfrog was following, but I pulled hard on his hand, which I still had tight hold of. "What's going on?" I asked in the lowest but sternest voice possible.

"We're getting help," he said quietly.

"Really? Other than being exhausted, what's the point of all of this?"

"Not being followed by enemies."

I decided refraining from comment was probably my best choice and let Bullfrog lead me out of the reed hut.

We exited onto a much nicer patch of land than we'd been on when we'd first entered this hut pathway. It was large enough to have held the Polliwog Palace. But there were no buildings here.

Thick, tall trees encircled the land, overrun with vines in a way that looked natural at first glance, but under closer examination were just a little too regular in places to be growing randomly. The vines wound tightly around and between the trees, which were close together in the first place. No one was going to get in, or out, through this living wall, unless they could climb really well.

What was here in place of a building or anything else, for that matter, was a nice little communications set up. It wasn't up to what a Diamante battle cruiser would have installed, but it looked at least as high quality as what we had on the *Stingray*—well, if you could get past the fact that everything seemed to be organically created.

Which I could because I'd been around the galaxy more than once.

It was just the three of us here that I could see. But again I figured there were plenty in the trees, watching.

What there weren't, though, were flies. None anywhere. I looked up. I wasn't positive, but it looked like there was a kind of fine netting connected to the tops of the tress, creating a lid on the area.

Another close look at the trees creating the walls of this place, and the same kind of netting or covering was on the inside "walls" of this very large room or facility or whatever Longdaddy considered it.

I looked at the communications center and revised my opinions. There weren't any Polliwogs in the trees, because the trees and vines were part of the overall organic computer system. This didn't mean there weren't guards of all kinds somewhere close – it just meant they weren't in the heart of the communications center.

Someone else came out of the hut we'd just left, presumably using the other staircase because I hadn't heard anyone behind us during our trek, and I'd been listening. I recognized her—one of the coat check girls from the Palace, the one who'd given Kyle her number. I tried not to worry about Roy and the others, let alone about Bullfrog and me, and failed utterly.

She bowed to Longdaddy. Once she straightened, he nodded. "What is the news, Lily?" he asked.

Lily grimaced. "Not much more than before. Based on today's events, the Leech is doing just as you suspected."

"And the others who went to visit the Leech today, how do they fare?"

"They're back on their ship, Longdaddy. Waiting."

"Waiting for what?" Bullfrog asked quietly.

Lily smiled at him. "Waiting for the two of you to return. Longdaddy, what else do you require?"

"Just remain watchful," he said as he put his hand on her head. "And remain faithful to our true ways."

"Always." Lily bowed, Longdaddy nodded, and she went back into the hut.

Longdaddy went to the main console and started fiddling with twigs and leaves and such, which altered the picture on the large screen that was made out of what I was pretty sure was spider silk.

Thinking about it, the "walls" and "ceiling" were probably lined with tight spider webbing. It was one of the more expensive of Arachnius' exports, meaning Longdaddy had more going on than being some sort of Swamp Swami.

There were a variety of options. I could stay quiet. I could try to run. Or I could ask the obvious. "What is it you suspect Monte the Leech of doing, Longdaddy?"

The screen came to life. It showed a solar system, or at least part of one. What was on the screen was rather desolate and seemed remote.

"Behold Orion's Light," Longdaddy said.

"That's the rock the Leech wants to build his Casino City on?" Bullfrog asked. "It doesn't even look like it's a moon."

I studied the space around Orion's Light. "I don't think it's a moon. It looks more like a giant asteroid that got lost from its belt."

"Who'd want to go there?" Bullfrog was asking the pertinent questions too.

Longdaddy turned and looked straight at us. "No one."

"So, why did you bring us here, to what I have to guess is the center of your operations, whatever they may be?"

Longdaddy looked at me for several long seconds. "I know what you really are."

Years of training to stay alive and safely hidden meant that instead of tensing, panicking, thinking thoughts that would give me away, or running like crazy, I remained calm and shrugged. "And what's that?"

Longdaddy smiled slowly, ensuring all his teeth showed. "You are, in some ways, like me. Hiding what you truly are." He turned back to the screen. The view moved out. It was clear Orion's Light had nothing much to recommend it—like a star close enough to warm it, for starters.

I decided to let his insinuation slide. "How did you get these pictures?"

"When Monte the Leech made a deal with the Diamante Families, that did not concern me much, even though I have people who travel to Roulette. When Monte the Leech came here, however, and then made another deal with the Underground, then I took an interest."

"I can understand that."

"When Monte the Leech hired many citizens to have an extra-good time at the Polliwog Palace 'undercover,' so to speak, I became *very* interested."

"Can't blame you. At all." Nice to have my suspicions confirmed.

"Thank you. However, when Monte the Leech proceeded to start discussing a new planetoid that would house yet another gambling world, I chose to take a much closer, more personal interest."

"The pictures on the screen indicate a pretty long range interest."

He shrugged. "We have more means and abilities than the Underground and the government might be aware of. And I used some of those means to send a trustworthy team to the coordinates being bandied about as the next gambling paradise."

"He might be terraforming it," Bullfrog offered, though he didn't sound like he'd bought into this idea. "Though it seems very far from anything that could warm it."

"It is too far away from Betelgeuse to receive much light, let alone heat."

"This is very interesting, but why are we here, specifically?"

Longdaddy turned again to us. "When a group of 'scientists' came into the Polliworld Palace, went to visit Monte the Leech, and then had to create a distraction of large proportions to escape, well, then I knew for certain the Jumping Game was on." He seemed just a little expectant.

"The Jumping Game is on" was an old Polliwog phrase. The Underground didn't use it, feeling it represented a more archaic time for their planet.

However, old or not, it was still used whenever something smelled, appeared, or felt off.

"We didn't create a distraction," Bullfrog lied. "We were attacked by the Underground."

Longdaddy gave him the kind of look a parent will give to a small child who's trying to blame something on the family pet — the "oh please, you expect me to fall for that one?" look. "Perhaps you are unclear about my abilities."

He fiddled with some twig knobs, and the picture on the screen changed. It showed the interior of the Polliwog Palace. Point of fact, it showed Bullfrog and me, imitating Ciarissa, causing havoc in the blackjack area.

"I wonder, Bullfrog. Where is the young lady you escaped the casino with? Surely you did not forget your upbringing and leave her alone and defenseless." Longdaddy zoomed in on me. Or, rather, me appearing to be Ciarissa.

Bullfrog cleared his throat. "Ah, no. I hid her...where DeeDee works."

Longdaddy rolled his eyes at me. "Let's see if you can do better."

I wanted to get us off the topic of what had happened to the "other girl." So I ran everything we'd experienced so far through in my mind and tried to think like Roy. "Monte's pulling a major land scheme, isn't he?"

Longdaddy's lips quirked. "I appreciate your attempt to distract." He nodded. "I believe the Leech is indeed trying to perpetrate a very risky scheme."

"Why do you care?"

Longdaddy cocked his head. "Why would *you* care?"

"I'd care because he's kind of our friend. He's playing the Diamante Families and the Polliworld Underground against each other. I get that it's a dicey game. But if they turned Monte into tomorrow's canapés for Oceana's Sharkfolk, why would *you* care?"

"Because the Leech would not be the only one affected."

Bullfrog cleared his throat again. He didn't do that often, so I figured he was at least as nervous as I was, maybe more so. This wasn't a comfort. "You think the Diamante Families will blame Polliworld? And...take action?" Which was a very diplomatic way of asking if Longdaddy felt the Diamante Families would declare another purge, focused solely on Polliworld. It certainly wasn't out of the realm of possibility.

"I believe this could happen, yes. Which is why I want you to fix it."

"Excuse me?" I managed to keep my voice somewhat level.

"I want you and the rest of your 'scientific team' to figure out a way to ensure that things stay...roughly the same."

"What if, despite the evidence, Monte's actually doing a legitimate business deal?"

Longdaddy gave me one of those "you're kidding, right?" looks. "What, in your experience with the Leech, would give you the impression he's not pulling a Jumping Game?"

I sighed. "Nothing. Look, before you threaten us with all the things you'll do to us and the rest of our team if we say no, I'd like to get some more information."

"What makes you feel you're in a position to bargain?"

"Really? We're going to play this game? Fine. We're in a position to bargain because you need us. If you didn't, we'd be dead in some way or another already." I glanced up at the sky again. "From the distance we traveled and the fact that you have this place insulated really well, and also based on when I know Monte's casino shifts normally change, we're a lot closer to Amphibia than you want us to know. My guess is that we're somewhere between the Space Center and the main part of town."

"Well done." Longdaddy turned to Bullfrog. "If I believed she was really a Polliwog, I would tell you to marry her."

"She's a Polliwog," Bullfrog said. "Just not from around here."

"No, I understand she is not from around here." He turned back to me. "You may ask your questions."

"Lucky me. So, why did the Diamante Families take part ownership in the Palace on Roulette?"

"Rumor has it that they were displeased with the Palace making more money on average than the Diamante Families casinos."

"Sounds like them. Why was the Underground willing to let Monte come here to open the Polliworld Palace?"

"Money."

"No other reason? You're sure?" Money seemed so...ordinary. Then again, who was I to complain about a simple goal?

"Yes, I'm quite sure. The Underground sees the casino as a way to allow them to expand off our planet."

"And Orion's Light is supposed to be their first expansion point, right?"

"Yes."

Time for the Big Question. "Who's aware that the Polliworld Palace isn't really in the black?"

Longdaddy appeared mildly impressed. I didn't know why. He'd shared this already, by confirming Monte had hired a lot of shills without the Underground's knowledge. "Only a few. The Leech has done a good job convincing the Underworld that things are going well."

"But you have people in the casino who know differently. Do you know how the Palace on Roulette is doing without Monte there?"

"The Palace was more profitable when it was being run by the correct being."

"Makes sense."

"Why isn't the Polliwog Palace doing well?" Bullfrog asked. "We Polliwogs love gambling."

Longdaddy shrugged. "We apparently love to travel to another world that is very different from our own when we are gambling. There is no allure to a casino that anyone and everyone can visit."

Interesting. I'd never have guessed that, and clearly Monte and the Underground hadn't guessed that, either. "Maybe over time it'll have an allure. How many spies do you have in the Underground?"

"Enough. Just as I have enough in the casino."

"And some in the Diamante Families, too, right?"

"Yes."

I took the logical leap. "The Diamante Families are also going in on Casino City, aren't they?"

Longdaddy smiled. "I would be willing to consider interspecies marriage."

"Flattery's a lot nicer than threats, so let's stick with that. Can we trust him?" I asked Bullfrog. "After we do what he wants, I mean."

I didn't expect an honest answer from Bullfrog. We were standing in front of Longdaddy, in his secret communications lair, without a lot of easy exit options. But I was very interested in Longdaddy's reactions to the question.

He laughed. And seemed unperturbed by the question and unworried about Bullfrog's reply.

Bullfrog shrugged. "Yes."

Longdaddy nodded. "Truthfully, you can trust me because I need to ensure that this problem is solved, and in the solving, that no blame can come back onto me and my people."

"Okay. Who are your people?"

"All those who hide in shadows. As you do."

"I don't hide in shadows."

Longdaddy smiled again, but this one was rather sad. "You do. Some shadows are transparent. But I understand that in order to survive you must lie to yourself. Oh, and since you asked before, I know you are not a Polliwog because one Polliwog went in to see the Leech...but two came out to No Frog's Land."

He turned back to the screen. I was still the main thing on view. Though, because I did excellent work, Ciarissa was still the main thing on view.

"I was on lookout at the rear entrance." I ensured I sounded bored. "Your spies must have missed me."

"Oh, they *believe* they missed you. In part because you count a very strong telepath as one of your friends."

This was getting creepy and spooky both. I wondered if Bullfrog had told Longdaddy about all of us, somehow.

"No idea what you're talking about."

Longdaddy shook his head. "We are having this conversation here because, as you noted, it is well insulated and protected. As you and so many others with you are hidden, so am I hidden, even from those who have known me all their lives. I am hidden until things will change so that I need not hide anymore."

He was giving me a clue, I was sure of it. Longdaddy was no longer talking about me, or even Ciarissa, because he'd said so many others. He was right—out of our crew, we had all of one being who wasn't hiding something in some way, and that was Willy. Sure, Bullfrog wasn't hiding that much, but he was pretending to be Underground in order to keep all of us safe. And get us jobs.

But Bullfrog wasn't the one Longdaddy was talking about hiding until things changed. Longdaddy had been here too long to be a hidden shifter, at least, that was my impression, and no hidden shifter would be offering another hidden shifter these kinds of clues. We had our ways of spotting the few of us who remained, and nothing Longdaddy had done was in line with those ways.

He wasn't a telepath or telekinetic, because Ciarissa had taught us how to tell if we were being read, and we weren't, and no one had tried to make our bodies do something we didn't want. Sure, he could be hiding either trait, but I just didn't think he was. So, did that mean he was referring to Roy and Kyle?

Polliworld, like most of the inhabiteds, had a long history. It had gone through turmoil several times before the Diamante Purge, but had survived because the Underground were already in power.

The answer came to me. "Polliworld used to be ruled by kings. But the Underground preferred a propped-up democracy over a monarchy because that gave them more ways to have power, especially if the current ruler was against them. The royal family disappeared. The general story is that they were smuggled off-world. But that's not the truth, is it?"

Longdaddy wouldn't have been born, or maybe was a tadpole, when the Underground took over Polliworld, because that had happened well before the Diamante Purge. Meaning he had a grudge against the Underground and the Diamante Families both. Just like Monte did. But unlike Monte, Longdaddy apparently had more to think of than himself. Just like Roy.

Longdaddy smiled. "It's good that we understand each other. You have proven yourself trustworthy to those in hiding," he said to Bullfrog. "I hope for the same trust for myself."

Bullfrog had lost his Polliwog stone face—awe and shock had taken over his expression—but he nodded. "Yes...sire."

Longdaddy shook his head. "Not now. Not officially. And not until such time as what your 'scientific team' truly works for is done."

"You're why we were able to come in so easily undercover!"

Longdaddy chuckled. "It helps to have friends in low places."

"And high ones. Okay, we're all on the same side, at least in grand, general terms. But if we're going to fix what's going on, we need more information."

"What else do you need?"

"A better understanding of just what's been going on, especially what Monte's done and promised. And safe passage back to our ship."

"Anything else?" Longdaddy asked.

"Yeah. Any suggestions you might have for how to solve your problem without getting exposed or killed, either you or us."

Longdaddy's smile widened. "I sense the beginning of a beautiful friendship."

Getting back to the *Stingray* involved more long walks through the underground hut path, but I'd been right—we were much closer to the Space Center than when we'd first entered No Frog's Land.

Bullfrog and I left Longdaddy well before the Space Center and were handed off from one Polliwog guide to another until we were back at the *Stingray*. Sure, we came into the docking bay via the employee's entrance, but otherwise it was a relatively normal return.

We were only going to be alone for a few seconds. "Bullfrog, did you tell Longdaddy about us? I won't be mad at you if the answer's yes, by the way."

"No, I didn't. I didn't know who he really was until we both found out today." Bullfrog rarely bothered to lie, and I was pretty sure he wasn't lying now.

"Huh. Okay. Well, good." Longdaddy knew who we were and what we were working for. And while all royalty knew or knew of each other somewhere and somehow, I doubted that King Oliver of Andromeda had been the one telling tales out of school.

Which meant someone else had told Longdaddy about us.

I considered this as we walked casually on board and were greeted with a lot of relieved expressions.

"Ciarissa said you two were okay, but I wasn't sure," Roy said as he hugged me tightly, even though I hadn't changed out of my Polliwog form.

"We're fine. We don't have a lot of time. Some big things need to happen, very publicly, in a short time from now."

"What?" Roy sounded ready for action. Pity.

"We can't actually tell you. Well, we can tell you some of what's going on, but not all. Not yet. I need Ciarissa, and you need to be ready to leave Polliworld the moment the two of us are back on the ship."

"What? You just got back and we weren't sure what we were going to have to do to retrieve you both safely. You are *not* leaving this ship without me, and that's final."

I heaved a sigh. "Come help me get into my Polliskin while we argue and you don't win. Oh, and Ciarissa, please get into your Polliskin, too."

She smiled serenely. "Of course, DeeDee."

We went to our quarters, and I changed back into me. Because it hadn't been necessary, I hadn't done a complete shift at any time. I hadn't moved my mind to the place where I didn't know who I was, because I *knew* I was someone else. The shifts had been short enough that I hadn't needed to. My mind was still fully my own, and therefore I didn't need to complete a full shifting ritual or use my Mantra of Self to return to being me.

Which was good, because despite the fact he was upset, Roy managed to kiss me deeply and remind me again why it was great to be his woman.

"Thanks for getting the taste of fly out of my mouth."

"I'd gag, but I know you didn't eat any. They have a distinct tang."

"And you know this how?"

Roy grinned. "You've had to eat flies before."

"Okay, you get to keep your special parts intact." I began struggling into the suit while Roy helped me.

"Good. What's going on?"

"I can't tell you. Yet. I can tell you once we finish helping Monte live up to his name."

"You don't mean you're going to be sucking someone's blood. Do you?" He sounded just a little worried. Too bad I didn't have time to laugh about this.

"No. I mean he's pulling the ancient three card monte routine, or as they call it here, the Jumping Game—but with land, not cards. And he's doing it with the biggest players around, thusly endangering everyone if things went wrong. Which they were, until we showed up."

"We're being played?"

"I don't think so. I think we've been recruited to be the third card, so to speak. And we'll be getting paid.

You just have to trust me and do exactly what Bullfrog and I tell you. And you have to let me and Ciarissa leave the ship. Alone. I promise we'll get back safely, and if we're in trouble, you'll know."

"Great. I hate it when you don't tell me what you're doing."

"Oh, I can tell you what I'm going to do. I'm rigging Monte's Jumping Game to ensure that it works and leaves everyone thinking they're the winners."

Ciarissa and I left the ship and headed into the Space Center. She was still wearing the head covering that made her look as if she was from Convent. I'd shifted to human male, big and imposing enough, without any clear planetary distinctions, in the kind of suit favored by both Underground and Diamante Families enforcers. However, this look was also fairly common on Convent.

We passed through the Spillway and went through customs via the Respite section. The clerk barely looked at us.

Once in the Space Center, we headed to the Swampland Zoo. "Why are we going here?" Ciarissa asked quietly.

"You know."

"You know I don't...access...anyone on the crew without their permission. Some strong thoughts reach me, yes, but I don't search for them. Speaking and reading are not the same things."

"I know." I paid to get in and headed us to the Wild Nature of Polliworld section. It was crowded with beings from all over. Good. I noted where the exits were, as well as which door said Employees Only. "So, we're going to admire the wild nature and you're going to tell me the nature of your relationship with Longdaddy." I watched her out of the corner of my eye. "Girl to girl."

There were enough people around, and we were speaking softly enough that it was unlikely we'd be overheard. Longdaddy had assured me that this section of the Swampland Zoo had its surveillance curtailed regularly.

"Ah. What do you think you know?"

"You're the one who told him about us."

"This is true." She moved off a few steps, as if we were honestly here to enjoy the exhibit. "He is trustworthy," she said when I was beside her again.

"I guessed. I don't think you're a traitor, because we'd all be dead already."

"No. I fight for what all of you fight for. He does as well."

"Yeah, I picked that up. How did you meet?"

"The usual way, I suppose."

"There are no usual ways anymore."

She chuckled. "True enough. I met him in the same way you met Roy. I was in over my head and he helped me."

"He's why you haven't given Doven the remotest go-ahead sign, isn't he?"

It was a rare thing, but I did get to bear witness to Ciarissa blushing. "In a way. We are only close friends."

"You and Longdaddy or you and Doven?"

"Both. While I would wish that circumstances were different, Longdaddy, as you call him, needs to ensure that his line, his pure line, continues. We both accepted that a long time ago."

"And Doven?"

"Why is this relevant?"

"Because it's the only time I'm ever going to get to ask without Roy or Doven or someone else overhearing. Because he's worried about you being worked too hard, but Roy's dismissed the idea, meaning that Roy doesn't think he's overtaxing you. But Doven feels you're overtaxed. Meaning you're keeping at least one being not on our crew advised of our activities and it's draining your strength." I looked straight at her. "I want to be sure of who you're telling what, when, and why."

She didn't turn toward me. "Much goes on while you are on assignment. The stirrings of what you and I are both trying to fix began well before your trip to Andromeda."

"How are you talking to Longdaddy when we're out of this solar system?"

"There are...ways." Now she did turn to me, and I could see the exhaustion in her eyes. I was sure Doven had seen this, and I was equally sure no one else had, because both Roy and Dr. Wufren would have put Ciarissa onto medical rest if they'd caught a whiff of this. "They can be quite...taxing."

"How many others are involved in those ways?"

"Fewer than you would think. It would be easier if there were more, but we are very spread out. All trustworthy. For the same reasons you are trustworthy."

"I want more than your word. I want the full explanation. I'm sorry, but under the circumstances, I can't trust you like I once did."

Ciarissa nodded sadly. "I understand. Once trust is lost..." She heaved a sigh. "Espen was spared destruction during the Purge because we have always taken the side of noninterference, of neutrality."

"You have laws about it, yeah. And, I'd assume, the Espen government has some way to control all of you."

"It does, other telepaths screening for overt activities mostly. But there are some of us who do not feel noninvolvement is always the ethical choice. During the Purge, we worked with many resistance fighters, trying to help them. For the most part, we failed."

"For the most part, everyone failed. But, how did you avoid anyone knowing about your involvement? Especially the Espen government?"

"The same way we avoid detection now. Longdaddy has some very advanced scientists who are quite loyal to him. They created a living organism that combined organically with those of us who continue to strive against the Diamante Families. The tad-biotic enhances our powers exponentially. It allows us to reach each other across the vast distances of space while helping to mask our activities and mental trails."

I'd seen Longdaddy's living computer system. It wasn't hard to believe that the beings responsible for that could create an organism that did what Ciarissa described. "Doctor Wufren, is he part of this, too?"

She shook her head. "Fren opposes the Diamante Families for the same reasons the rest of you do, but he was never a part of the Espen Resistance. He self-exiled from Espen well before the Purge."

Interesting. Yet another fact I hadn't known. Roy might not know, either. "How many of you are there?"

"Not enough, but we do what we can. We are placed within certain organizations, on specific planets, within groups where our assistance is most needed."

The light dawned. "That's why you fly with us."

She smiled. "I would fly with you even if I was not part of the Espen Resistance. I requested to be given the chance to join with Roy and his loyal retainers." Her expression saddened. "I have lost many things because of the Purge and my planet's refusal to help fight against obvious evil. I don't want to lose your trust, or lose the family I have joined and love."

Had to give one thing to the Diamante Families— they really brought a galaxy together, united under the banners of loathing, hatred, and revenge.

Maybe I should have continued to be suspicious, but I'd known Ciarissa a long time now. Having met Longdaddy, it was clear that we were all on the same side. Besides, I didn't want to lose anyone or anything else because of the Diamante Families.

I hugged her. "I understand."

Her body relaxed against mine, and Ciarissa hugged me back tightly. "I would prefer not to tell the others about any of what we have discussed."

"Let's get out of this situation first, and then worry about who gets to know what."

"What situation are we in, exactly?"

Either she was faking it really well, or Ciarissa truly hadn't been reading me and Bullfrog while we were gone, other than at a very high level. While I was ready to forgive her, there was information I needed to have in order to ensure our crew's long term health and happiness.

"We're here to save the day again. Per my intel, it should pay well. *If* we can pull it off. But we're not going to pull it off until you tell me if Doven's interest in you really is or isn't returned."

Ciarissa stared at me for a few long moments. "You would endanger an entire world for this information?"

"Yeah, I would. But I don't think you would."

She shook her head. "That is not like you."

"Based on what I've learned today, you aren't like you. Not the you we thought you were. So why does it surprise you that I might be different than you've thought?"

"Because I've seen your true heart, as I've seen the true hearts of all who fly with us. It is *why* I fly with all of you. And because of this, I know you will not risk the lives of innocents on a whim."

"It's not a whim. Doven and Roy are fighting because of you, and we can't afford to have that. I need to know, right now, where your loyalties — romantic and otherwise — really lie."

"My loyalties are with the Martian Alliance. I believe bringing back the true galactic emperor, especially as personified in Roy, will be what the galaxy truly needs. The Espen Resistance agrees with this — they want a return to the former rulerships, kingdoms, democracies, theocracies, and such that existed before the Diamante Families took over."

"Good to know. And your romantic loyalty — is it to Doven, Longdaddy, someone else, or no one else?"

"Ah. You fly with the man you love, so you need to know if it's the same for me?"

I rolled my eyes. "I'd fly with Roy even if I didn't love him, and vice versa. You're stalling, waiting for someone to come and interrupt us. But I have a guarantee of privacy, because Longdaddy understands what my price for participation is. So, stop dancing around the question and answer me — do you have romantic feelings for Doven like he has for you?"

She looked straight into my eyes. "No."

"Fair enough." I stepped closer to the Employees Only door.

Ciarissa joined me. "That's it? No protests, no pushing me to give Doven a chance? No coercion in any way?"

"No. I just wanted to know. So I won't encourage him to actually bird up and ask you out. I thought he was reading you wrong, but I guess he's right — his love is unrequited."

A quick look around showed that no one was really paying attention to us. I went to the Employees Only door. As promised, it opened right up. I stepped through, motioning to Ciarissa to follow me.

She did and we started down a hallway that looked a lot like the hallway in the Polliwog Palace that led to Monte's office.

Ciarissa put her hand onto my arm. "You misunderstand me. I answered your specific question. I don't have romantic feelings for Doven like he has for me. Our differences mean we can never feel exactly the same way about each other."

"Oh, good grief. Stop being coy. I need to focus. Do you want to date and potentially mate with Doven or not?"

"I...would be willing."

"Great." There was supposed to be a hidden entrance somewhere around here. It was really well hidden. "Then, when we're done with this, make the first move. He's never going to. I realize you've probably been waiting for him to actually talk to you about this. I also realize, having met Mister I Advertise, that Longdaddy undoubtedly made a move within the first five minutes of meeting you. Doven's not like that. He's got all that rigid morality up in his feathers and he's convinced himself you're not interested. He's as likely to make a move on you as I am to come on to Monte."

"Oh. Uh, thank you."

"Any time. We'll worry about how to get you more rest so Doven stops stressing out about your exhaustion later. Right now, we need to roll on our part of the latest plan I wanted no part of, and I can't get us out of this stupid hallway. There's a hidden door around here. Any guess as to where it is?"

"Yes." Ciarissa walked us a few more feet and then pointed down. "There is a stairway here." She pushed what looked like a screw, and a portion of the floor raised just enough to be able to lift it.

"Of course there is. What a world, what a world."

Ciarissa headed down the dark stairs. I went after her, ensuring the trapdoor was securely closed behind us.

"How many times have you used this path?" I asked.

"Never. I just knew what to look for."

We reached the bottom. This walk wasn't nearly as long or steep as those Bullfrog and I had taken during our Swamp Walk. I was going to sleep for a week once this caper was over. And demand that Roy give me leg rubs...so, maybe I wouldn't sleep the entire time.

We came to a three-way fork in the path. A small arsenal was piled onto a wheelbarrow. Per what Longdaddy had told me, I knew to take the rightmost path. The curiosity to see where the other paths led almost overwhelmed me. Then I remembered that all roads led to either flies or Longdaddy's lair, my legs hurt in any form I shifted into, and I didn't want to stay on Polliworld any longer than we had to. I grabbed the wheelbarrow and made the hard right.

When we came to the next set of steps leading up, I shifted again. This time, I ensured that I was very recognizable.

Ciarissa's eyes, like mine, had adjusted to the dark – I knew because she jumped. "Is this a wise gambit?"

"Yes. It helps that you're disguised to look like you're from Convent. We need to have someone to blame, and that blame can't come back on any of us, on Longdaddy or Polliworld, and not on Monte, either. This is the best option." Plus, I was fairly sure Monte was betting on us using this gambit or something close to it. He wasn't a stupid being in any way, and he knew us pretty darned well.

"They're going to try to kill us the moment they see you."

"That's why you're along. Feel free to exhaust yourself. I can carry you back to the ship if needed."

"I didn't hide my past relationship to keep something from you or Roy or the others. Roy doesn't announce who he truly is and what organization he supports to just anyone, either. But until one of you met Longdaddy, there was no reason to advise that another monarch was closer to his throne than the Diamante Families might realize."

"I'm not upset with you." Anymore.

Ciarissa shook her head. "Yes, you still are, at least a little bit. I thought we'd already made our peace." She sounded sad and worried.

"We have." I sighed. "I need to be angry, because it's going to help me stay in character. So, let me stay angry with you for right now, because it's a fresh anger, so it's easier to tap into and maintain. Once we're back on the *Stingray*, I'll be back to me. In all ways. Deal?"

"Deal."

"Great. Then let's go show everyone that the boogeyman is alive and well and seriously pissed."

We took the various armaments Longdaddy had provided. We were both weighed down with a lot of firepower—me more than Ciarissa, but then, I could carry a lot in this form. And we were going to need to put on a very effective show for this to work.

The stairs led right to the back hallway behind Monte's office, just as Longdaddy had said they would. I had to give it to him—he'd really set things up well. I wondered how much Ciarissa had told him about us, and figured a lot. So, Longdaddy and Monte were both counting on us doing exactly what we were about to do.

By now, Bullfrog should have told Roy what was going on, other than about Ciarissa, because I didn't think he'd made the connection about her relationship with Longdaddy, or if he had, he hadn't shared it with me. But either way, it was safe to assume the *Stingray* had left Polliworld very officially and that the *Redeemer's Will* was going to return shortly, guns blazing.

It was dangerous, so dangerous, for me to do this particular shift. But there didn't seem to be any other way. At least not a way that would leave everyone I cared about safe. Roy had no idea how dangerous a shift this would be for me, either, but I knew he wouldn't like it, just on general principles. Which was why I'd ensured Ciarissa and I were already too far away to alter the plan before Bullfrog explained what we were doing.

Roy wasn't really like Roman. Maybe a little like Roman—very male, very captivating, and a great leader. Okay, so Roy was a lot like Roman in those ways. But Roy would never intentionally kill an innocent, no matter what the cause or the cost. And should that happen, he'd never wave it away as the cost of war. Roy understood the cost of war, but he didn't enjoy spending the money. Roman, on the other hand, felt quite differently.

For Roman, it was his way or the highway to Hell.

Longdaddy's people were already in place and ready, he'd assured me of that, and I'd watched him send the message, which was why we had to ensure we timed everything right. Longdaddy had also verified there was no life on Orion's Light. And I'd shared what I'd do to him if I discovered that was a lie. So all was set.

Ciarissa nodded. "Monte is alone, but all the surveillance is active."

"Showtime," I said quietly. In this form, my voice was deep, low, and had a very charismatic quality. I'd ensured I'd shifted everything, including matching Roman's mind. I was able to do so because I'd known him personally. I'd known him better than anyone, and certainly better than anyone still alive.

Being angry with Ciarissa was helpful because Roman had been a very angry person. His voice hadn't been the only charismatic thing about him, either. Hopefully I radiated his machismo, because if I didn't put on a believable show, we were all dead.

But the time for doubts was over. I finalized the shift in my mind.

I looked around, taking in the scene. I wasn't that old a man, but sometimes my life's experiences made me feel ancient. My memory liked to disappear occasionally. It was a test—of my faith, my strength, and my conviction. I closed my eyes and centered on the beating of my heart. Ah, yes. I never failed this test. Because my cause was righteous and I could not, would not, be stopped.

Memory flooded back, as it always did. I was Roman the Redeemer, here with one of my loyal adherents to stop anyone from overtaking yet another defenseless world against its will. Orion's Light would not fall into the hands of Diamante scum. Better they should burn in righteous fire than fall to the most evil and godless of empires.

"Tell our allies to begin."

Ciarissa nodded. An explosion rumbled – the sound, and the screams, confirmed it was close by. More explosions, more screaming, both within the building and outside. The *Redeemer's Will* must have made itself known.

We went to the office's rear door. I contemplated knocking, but that wasn't a frightening enough entrance. And this fool needed frightening. At the very least. I kicked the door in. The wood splintered in a satisfying manner.

I shoved Ciarissa back and to the side as I jumped out the way. Sure enough, lasers fired at us. I was used to guerilla fighting, however.

I tossed in a gas bomb, courtesy of our local allies. It was non-lethal, which was something of a disappointment. But agreements had been made and compromises were sometimes necessary.

I strode in to see a variety of Underground personnel on the ground and Monte the Leech gaping at me. Due to his nature, he was unaffected by the gas—his kind could simply absorb it through their skin and eject it later as excrement. "You...you're alive?"

"You won't be for too long." I nodded to Ciarissa, and she concentrated. The bodies convulsed then went still. Enforced comas. They'd recover in a few days. If we didn't blow this den of iniquity sky high first.

"What have *I* done?" Monte asked, looking around wildly.

"Guards are coming, as are both more Underground and Diamante Families enforcers. I have alerted the Redeemer's Will."

"You will not defile Orion's Light. There is enough sin in this galaxy already."

"S-Sorry. But, the plans are set. Casino City will be beautiful to behold."

"Can you see Orion's Light from here?"

Monte nodded.

"Show me."

"The Redeemer's Will has created a disturbance, adding to the existing explosions and chaos. There is panic in the streets, which has spilled into the casino. Guards and enforcers are delayed."

He undulated over to the wall with the drawing of Casino City and pushed a button. The picture slid up, revealing a holoscreen. The rock named Orion's Light floated in the center. "There it is."

"Some guards and enforcers have made it through and will be here momentarily."

I could hear the sounds of destruction coming closer. There were a lot of beings causing quite the ruckus. Good.

I set myself between Ciarissa and the door, guns ready. "You will agree to cease all plans for your defilement of Orion's Light, or I will remove the temptation for you."

The first of the Diamante Families personnel breached the doorway. I shot him dead, and the three behind him. "Toss your weapons into the room, or I'll send you all to the fire!"

Some weapons were tossed in. So was a grenade. I picked it up and tossed it back. Because of my size, everyone always underestimated my speed and agility. To their detriment. The explosion was muffled by the bodies. No loss. No one in this den of iniquity would be worth redeeming, other than by blood and fire.

"If any of you still live, send a message to your employers—I will not allow Orion's Light to be defiled. I will burn this world if you continue trying to extend your sin to others."

"A few still live, and they are running away. They know who you are, and their terror of you is much more than their terror of what their own masters will do to them. They will share your message."

I turned back to the Leech. "You will cease all your plans with Orion's Light."

"Hardly. Look, Roman, can I call you Roman? Roman, this is a business deal."

"Burn your contracts before me."

"They're in a safe place, Roman. I can't access them at this precise time. Especially since I think you blew up my storage area."

This I knew to be a lie. However, there were other ways. "Then prepare to have those contracts declared null and void."

"No can do, Roman. They're ironclad."

I shrugged and looked at Ciarissa. "Then we go with Plan B."

"Plan B?" Monte asked nervously. "What's Plan B?"

Ciarissa was concentrating. I could tell by her expression and the look in her eyes.

"You'll see." Ciarissa nodded and closed her eyes. I picked her up in my arms. "I will let you live today, Leech, because there is a chance, however slim, that you may be redeemed. But if you try to claim another planet or moon as you have Orion's Light, I will return and feed you to the fire."

"Plan B is you leaving?" Monte asked hopefully.

I nodded toward the holoscreen. "That is Plan B."

Right on cue, Orion's Light exploded into a million tiny pieces.

"Guards!" Monte screamed. "Guards!"

"They are dead or gone." I heard the sound of coordinated marching coming closer. The Diamante Families must have gotten themselves in order. "As are all who oppose their Redeemer."

I strode from the room. Once out of the Leech's sight, I ran the way we'd come. We reached the trapdoor and were down it quickly, even with my having to carry Ciarissa. We raced down the stairs, her still in my arms, and then down the dark tunnel.

Lily was waiting for us at the fork. "Come this way." She turned and ran down the leftmost fork, and we followed.

After a long run we slowed to a walk. "I can stand," Ciarissa said. I put her down and we continued on after Lily.

About an hour later we reached another set of stairs. Lily stopped. "You need to stay here. The *Redeemer's Will* has been run off by several Diamante Families cruisers, but it did escape destruction. Wait until dawn, then you can go up. Once there, we will shuttle you to your ship." She bowed. "Thank you for your help, Roman the Redeemer." She handed Ciarissa a small bag.

I nodded and she left the way we'd come. Ciarissa and I sat on the steps.

"You should change back," she said softly.

"To what?"

"To your true self. There will be no shuttle. The Redeemer's Will is long gone."

"Get out of my head."

Ciarissa looked worried. She rummaged through the bag and relief washed over her face. She pulled out a small mirror and handed it to me. "Look at this."

I did. I looked tired. Leading a resistance took a lot out of a man.

"Your name is Danielle Daniels. Your friends call you DeeDee. You were born on Seraphina and carry part of it within your body and soul. You're part of the crew of a ship known only to said crew as the Hummingbird. Your life is your own, your loyalty is to those you love and those you serve."

As I looked and listened to the words in my head, I remembered that she was right. A part of me didn't want to, but I shifted back into myself. A redheaded woman in a Polliskin who looked tired—but not as tired as the man—stared back at me.

Ciarissa put her arm around my shoulders. "You're safe to say it aloud."

"How did you know it?"

"Roy asked me to memorize it in case you ever...forgot...when he wasn't nearby."

Staring at the mirror, I repeated the Mantra of Self, and my mind shifted fully back to what it should be. "It was a short shift. It shouldn't have been this hard to come back."

"Ah. How well did you know Roman?"

"Why do you assume I knew him?"

"You couldn't have imitated him so well if you didn't know him. And...at least a part of you didn't want to come back from being him."

I stared at myself. It was so easy to be Roman. He never had any doubts. Even when he was wrong—horribly, terribly, evilly wrong—he never doubted himself, his actions, or his choices. There was a kind of peace in that kind of blind belief. But that was only part of why I hadn't wanted to come back.

"You're right. I didn't want to come back." I leaned my head against hers. "But I'm happy to be back, so thank you."

"It's what friends are for." Ciarissa hugged me again. "What was he to you?"

"Oh, I guess he was my Longdaddy. In a way, at any rate."

"Will you tell me about it? One day?"

"Yeah, but only if you tell me about Mister I Advertise." We sat there for a few minutes in silence. "Roy is a better man than Roman ever was. Because Roy questions his motivations. And because Roy would never kill an innocent intentionally, even if he was trying to prove a point."

"Just as you wouldn't. Which is why I fly with the same crew you do. I have my own Mantra of Self. So does Fren. So do all the others. In our own ways."

"Was anyone hurt?"

"No one innocent. Longdaddy's people ensured that the civilians were protected and ushered to safety.

The bombs blew up areas with no one there. As planned." She pointedly didn't mention the grenade and I pointedly didn't ask about it. Those who worked protection for the Underground and Diamante Families weren't innocent.

"Good. I want to go home."

"I as well. Our home is currently waiting for the time just before dawn, when no one is truly alert and it's very difficult to see well."

"Did Lily lie about the shuttle?"

"No. There will be a shuttle waiting to take Roman the Redeemer to his ship. Only he will not come and so his legend will grow. Again."

"How are we going to get off this rock?"

Ciarissa stood up and offered me her hand. "We're going back the way we came. You won't need to shift again. The late night shift at the Space Center isn't manned with the most alert personnel."

We held hands all the way back. It was good to feel the connection to someone, and I needed it. That Ciarissa knew, too, was a given.

The stairs finally appeared, and we climbed them. We walked out the Employees Only door and wandered through the Zoo. We had a little time to kill. The Zoo was open around the clock, because while Polliwogs had regular sleep schedules, they weren't against visitors spending their currency the moment their ships docked.

Once we'd stared at the exhibits enough, we left and headed back to the Spillway. I had a moment's worry that someone would ask us what ship we were going to, but we sailed through without any interest from anyone. Either Longdaddy had a really long reach, Ciarissa was doing something to everyone's minds, or the staff were as lax as advertised. I decided not to care.

To my pleasant surprise, the *Stingray* was waiting for us. It looked as if it has just landed.

The ramp lowered and Roy came out. "About time. I hope us leaving you here has taught you two a lesson. You two need to spend less time gambling. You might have been killed in that attack. If we'd waited any longer for you, we might have been blown up."

Ciarissa looked down. "Sorry, sir."

I followed suit. "Sorry. We're okay. We were at the Space Center when it started. We were frightened, so we stayed until it seemed safe and we knew you were back."

"Oh, just get in. We need to get our samples home as quickly as possible," Roy snapped.

We trotted inside. Roy closed the ramp, grabbed my hand, and headed us for the cockpit. "Crew, strap in!"

Doven had the engines running, and as soon as Roy was in the captain's seat, we took off. I almost fell, but Doven reached back, caught me, and helped me into my seat.

We made escape velocity, and after a great deal of Roy and Doven muttering back and forth about the appropriate jumps to take to ensure no one was on our tail, they calibrated and we did the jump.

My stomach turned inside out and over, and shared that if I'd had any food in it, said food would be in the cockpit. "I don't feel so good." The extra pressure of hyperspeed was pressing down on me more than normal.

"I knew you wouldn't," Roy said. "That's why we're going to fly at regular speeds once we come out of this jump. Which will be right about now."

Sure enough, my stomach flipped again, and then the pressure was gone. We were in the middle of nowhere, space-wise, which sounded just fine right about now.

"You have this?" Roy asked Doven, who nodded. Roy got up, got me out of my seat, and carried me to our room. "You did a lot of work on this one, babe. You could have let us back you up more."

"No, you did what we needed. I'm just glad the ship wasn't damaged."

"Well, if Doven couldn't do what he does, it would have been a near thing. But the laser shots went wide. We're good. You look exhausted." Roy started to get me out of my Polliskin—help I didn't object to at all.

"Yeah. I feel that way, too. Ciarissa probably does as well."

"I hope it was all worth it," Roy said worriedly. "I know you said we were getting paid, but there's no proof we can trust our 'employer' to follow through. Though, thankfully, from what we were able to glean, no one was hurt, other than minor things like cuts and bruises."

"Trust me, some were hurt."

He grinned. "Well, no one innocent. I know that a few Diamante enforcers took some damage, at the hands of some Underground enforcers, who also took some damage from the Diamante enforcers."

"I enjoy a good, especially a fight where everyone getting hit is someone I dislike." I considered telling Roy about the enforcers I'd killed, but that could lead to questions I wasn't ready to answer. "But, trust me, we're getting paid. We know things about our employers they don't want spread about."

"Employers plural? I thought we were just getting paid by that Longdaddy guy."

So Bullfrog hadn't told Roy who Longdaddy really was. Fair enough. Secrets could destroy, but they could also protect. As long as we got paid, I was willing to protect Longdaddy's secret. Preserving that secret meant we'd keep him as an ally. I'd learned long ago that you could never have too many allies.

"Employers plural, yeah. We should hear from them shortly."

"What do you want to do until then?" Roy asked as he helped me into a flight robe.

"Honestly? I'm starving."

He grinned and picked me up. "Then let me take you to the galley."

"I love you." I kissed him deeply, all the way to the galley, which wasn't nearly long enough.

Everyone other than Doven was with us in the dining room. Tresia had made up a great breakfast, sandworms included. Ciarissa and I were eating like we'd never seen food before, but no one else was making Tresia doubt her cooking skills either.

"It was dicey," Willy said, "using Roman the Redeemer."

"But always effective," Dr. Wufren countered.

"We needed blame to fall on someone and it had to be someone who wasn't innocent," Bullfrog explained. "Can't think of anyone better than the Redeemer."

"As long as he doesn't know we're impersonating him," Willy muttered.

I chose not to mention that this particular worry was a moot point, and Ciarissa didn't add that, either. Another secret, now known by more than just me— Roman the Redeemer was dead. I'd referred to him in the past tense and Ciarissa had noted that slip. But she didn't know the full truth about Roman or his death. I wasn't ready to share that with anyone, not even Roy. In some ways, least of all Roy. Roy wouldn't understand why a part of me still loved Roman, even though I'd had to kill him in cold blood.

Doven's voice came through the intercom system. "Roy, we just received two coded transmissions, both from Polliworld."

"What do they say?"

"Not much. One's just a deposit confirmation for our account on Espen. To the tune of fifty thousand galaxy credits. No depositor is listed."

There were the usual gasps and whistles. I spent the time eating more sandworms.

So Longdaddy had some serious financial reserves. Good to know. I didn't figure we'd drained his account, but I did figure he wanted us happy with him in case he needed us again. Plus I was sure he wanted to take care of Ciarissa.

"What's the other message?" Roy asked.

"Copies of some contracts. I downloaded them to the dining room's reader."

Roy got up and looked at the screen on the wall that separated the galley from the dining room. "Huh. These are Monte's contracts with the Underground and the Diamante Families." He started to laugh.

"What?" Kyle asked. "Tell us."

I swallowed my last sandworm. "Longdaddy's people hacked Monte's system ages ago, so they've seen these contracts...therefore, Bullfrog and I got to see them, too. There are Act of Galaxy, Act of Gods, and Act of Terrorism clauses in those contracts. Should all or part of Orion's Light be destroyed or so damaged by any of those Acts, then all monies paid are forfeited. In other words, if the Diamante Families paid Monte a million credits for their part of Casino City, since Roman the Redeemer's people destroyed Orion's Light, those monies are forfeit. And Monte keeps them."

"DeeDee's right," Roy said. "There's a ten percent good faith return clause, which means Monte gives them ten percent back and pockets the rest." He turned around. "We were always part of the scheme, weren't we?"

"Yeah, I think so. You need three cards to play three card monte, after all. And Monte knows us well."

"You took a real risk, though, little girl." Willy looked worried. "Monte knows you shifted into the Redeemer. What if he finds a way to tell the Redeemer about that? Could put the Redeemer after you." Nice to know that Roman's boogeyman reputation was alive and well everywhere.

"No," Ciarissa said. "Monte now believes we call Roman the Redeemer an ally. He also believes the only reason he still lives is because we asked the Redeemer to spare him."

We all looked at her. She shrugged. "I can talk in anyone's mind, you know." She cleared her throat. "I also told him that if we didn't get twenty percent, then we were going to have to tell the Redeemer that Monte had reneged on his part of the deal."

"We just got another deposit notice," Doven shared. "Four hundred thousand credits, yet another anonymous donor."

"But twenty percent of a million is two hundred thousand," Roy said.

I finished my drink. "Yes, but Monte had a deal with the Underground, too. Now he can buy out their shares of the casinos as another goodwill gesture. He owns both casinos free and clear and he's out from under both the Underground and the Diamante Families."

We all sat there quietly for a few moments. "Well," Roy said finally, "if we're going to be used in someone else's con, at least the payoff was worth it."

I stood up and stretched. "Truly. Now, I'm really tired. Roy, take me to bed. And, Ciarissa, why don't you keep Doven company, just in case he's feeling sleepy."

She smiled, back to her usual serene demeanor. "Absolutely, DeeDee. Willing to have some company, Doven?" she asked.

"Certainly," Doven replied. "Turning intercom off now."

"Good choice," I said under my breath as Ciarissa headed for the cockpit, and Roy and I headed for the bedroom.

"What?"

I looked up at him. "I said I made a good choice when I met you, Roy."

He smiled. "Then let me make sure you still think so."

We went to bed a lot richer in money, knowledge, and secrets. It wasn't enough to take down the Diamante Families yet, but every successful job got us closer—even jobs we didn't know we were taking.

Roy slid under the sheet next to me. "Now, babe, let me show you how I play three card monte. I do it a little differently from everyone else."

True enough, and as with everything else Roy did, it was the best.

A Bug's Life

GINI KOCH

"Asteroid shower!" Roy's voice came over the intercom. "Crew to stations and strap in!"

When you're flying in deep space, there are few things that scare you more than being caught in an asteroid shower. Because even a small rock can rip a hole in your hull, and any hole that isn't immediately patched has the potential to destroy the spaceship and all the life within it.

Our stations during an asteroid shower were different than for any other type of flying experience. Sure, Roy was a fantastic pilot. And the chances of him avoiding most of the rocks were high. But they weren't a hundred percent. We scrambled.

Once in position, we were all standing up, really tethered more than strapped in, each against a padded interior wall -- concussions tended to slow a being down, and if an asteroid breached, slow was not the best option. But we controlled how far our tethers could release. Until necessary, "not at all" was the operative choice. Everyone also had a patch kit in hand and ready to go.

"Intercom is open. Crew report, please," Doven, our Quillian co-pilot and navigator said. "In station order."

"Engineering strapped," Willy shared. "No damage at this time. Engines running fine. Kyle's with me." Willy was our ship's engineer. Kyle was Roy's younger brother and basically making it a point to learn every station on the crew, just in case. And in cases such as this, Roy always wanted two in Engineering anyway.

"Medical strapped, all's well here," Dr. Wufren said.

"Quarters strapped," I said. "Ciarissa, Bullfrog and I are in, doors are open, no signs of damage." Our living quarters required the most beings to watch them, as we had a crew of nine and had ten rooms, total. Two of them weren't used currently, because Roy and I slept together. However, ten rooms, two group bathrooms, and a connecting hallway took more than one being to watch. If Roy hadn't wanted two in Engineering, we'd have definitely wanted Kyle with us up in Quarters.

"General Areas strapped," Tresia said. Normally, we'd want another crew member in General Areas as well, but Tresia was an Arachnidan. Eight-limbed beings had an advantage when it came to patching holes quickly, and Tresia was extremely quick. She said being our galley chef made her fast, but it probably had more to do with the speed and agility exercises she performed daily.

Which was a good thing, because even though Roy had the *Hummingbird* whirling like a dervish, we still took damage. We all heard the *pingggg* sound. I couldn't speak for the others, but my whole body tensed. Then there were more *pinggggs*.

"Got it!" Tresia called. Cheerfully. I hadn't asked her, but I always felt that Tresia actually enjoyed the danger asteroid showers presented.

"There were at least five hits," Roy said, voice tight.

"Six," Tresia corrected. "All in the same area. Patching them all at once was easier than making breakfast, Roy. And before you ask, I'm ready with six more patch kits."

"Good. We're not through this yet."

Everyone managed to refrain from stating that we knew we were still in danger. The *Hummingbird* spinning and flipping was sort of a clue. Strapped or not, from the sounds most of us were making, we were all really testing out the padding at our stations. Tresia, however, was humming. Yeah, she really loved these moments. Clearly Roy wasn't letting her see enough action.

More *pinggggs*. Not good. Roy was usually far better at avoiding hits than this. "Got them!" Tresia called.

"Engineering took one hit," Kyle said. "It's patched. You gonna ever get us out of this, big bro?"

"It's a gigantic shower," Doven replied, voice tenser than Roy's had been. "I see no end to it."

"Then how did we get into it in the first place, if it's that big?" Bullfrog asked as we took another hit that he leapfrogged to and patched. Since he was a Polliwog, he really did leap. Like a frog. Having him stationed in Quarters was a big reason why we were able to cover with just three of us.

"There is nothing of this on our navigational charts," Doven said. "And we have the most recent updates."

"It came out of nowhere," Roy said. "Just be glad we weren't at warp when we hit this. Hang on. Heading for one of the giant rocks."

"That never ends well," I pointed out as we took another hit, near me, this time. I slammed the metal patch over the hole and welded it shut in just a few seconds. Then I looked for the rock that had made said hole.

And found it.

And discovered something unsettling – it wasn't a rock.

"Roy, abort that plan!"

"What?"

"Don't go into whatever it is you see ahead of us. We need to get out of this, but don't get into it even more."

"Why not?" Doven asked. "We can shelter from the smaller rocks inside the larger one."

"It's not a rock. It's a ship. Well, what's left of a ship."

"How can you tell?" Roy asked. "You're in Quarters. Are you looking out a porthole?"

"No. I can tell because I'm holding the object that came through the hull near to me, and it's not a rock. It's a rivet." I looked at the rivet more closely. "In fact, I think it's a Pillar rivet."

"I've searched for what broke through in the Galley," Tresia said. She no longer sounded cheerful. "I also have metal pieces, and they are absolutely Pillar design."

"I sense no minds other than ours," Ciarissa said grimly.

"Roy, I'll try to create a telekinetic shield," Dr. Wufren said. "Not sure how long I can hold it, my boy, but now that I know what we're in the midst of, I can at least make the attempt."

"You're sure?" Roy asked, sounding concerned. Dr. Wufren normally didn't expend his telekinesis talent on meteor showers because for him to create this kind of shield took a lot of energy and, in case a big rock made it through, his talent was our last line of defense to keep us from ripping apart.

"Yes," Dr. Wufren said firmly. "The danger is confirmed greater than normal. What we're in the midst of could rip us to shreds much more effectively than your average asteroid shower."

"What *are* we in the midst of?" Kyle asked.

I had the answer. It wasn't a good answer, but we were all used to that. "Genocide."

The Diamante Purge had focused on races and sub-species of races that had greater powers than the norm. The only planet filled with special beings left alone was Espen – where Ciarissa and Dr. Wufren were from – a planet filled with beings with a variety of tele-talents. The generally accepted reason why Espen had been spared was that they had a strict noninterference policy and they policed their people better than anyone else could.

The rest of us weren't so lucky. Quillians with Shaman Powers, which Doven possessed, were almost completely wiped out. Shape shifters such as myself were even rarer. Doven and I had both survived because we were the best as what our races did and we were smart survivors. And because we'd joined with Roy.

Roy and Kyle were as rare as Doven and I were; not for their special powers, but for their bloodline. They were from the Martian Imperious line, meaning that Roy was the true Galactic Emperor. Not that anyone other than the crew of the *Hummingbird* and a select, trustworthy few knew this.

The Diamante Families had done their best to destroy not only the Imperious bloodline, but all the existing governments – monarchies, democracies, theocracies, and so on – so that every being in the galaxy would bow to one name and one name only.

Millions died in the Purge, but most still had planets to call home. Not all, of course. I was among those who would never, ever be able to return home – the shifter home planet of Seraphina had been turned into an asteroid belt by the power of the Diamante Families and their weapons of horrific destruction.

The planet of Pilla had also been destroyed. However, the Pillar had no special talents that made the Diamante Families jealous or wary. They were an insectoid race – and unlike the Arachnidans, who, per Willy, resembled a cross between Old Earth grasshoppers, beetles, and spiders – Pillars weren't remotely threatening.

Arachnidans had eight limbs complete with pincers, were tall and could be imposing, and could move deceptively fast. Among their many talents, they were excellent hand-to-hand and weapons fighters, fabulous dancers and artists, and, as Tresia proved daily, excellent chefs.

By comparison, Pillars were long, but not tall. They possessed a brittle shell and fifty tiny legs. When threatened, they curled up into balls. This was effective because their brittle shells became hard as iron when they were in a ball. It was ineffective in that they weren't able to do much other than roll – if they'd curled up on an incline. They were good scientists and mathematicians, however, their species focus was on their own planet and people and doing their best to be left alone.

Their main contribution to the galaxy was music. Pilla had the most accomplished musicians of any planet – fifty little legs could do amazing things with a piano, a drum set, a violin, or anything else. They were mostly useless on woodwinds, though some Pillars did manage to master them, and those who did were always exceptional.

There was no logical reason for the Diamante Families to destroy this planet. Pilla had nothing impressive in terms of natural resources, no solar- or galactic-level weapons of any kind, a desire to just stay on Pilla and be ignored, and a planetary belief that the power of music was all a being needed to make the galaxy better. When a being looked up the definition of "nonthreatening" a picture of a Pillar would be shown.

But destroy Pilla the Diamante Families did, as viciously as they destroyed Seraphina. However, they didn't destroy the Pillars. Because the Pillars had been warned somehow, and the entire population was off planet when the Diamante Families' Destruction Fleet arrived. The general assumption was that the Espen Resistance had given the Pillar leadership the head's up that it was time to run, but this had never been proven.

Due to their brittle shells, the Pillar were unable to travel in warp – the pressure of traveling at warp speed would crush them flat. They could go into what they called Round Form and survive, but they couldn't remain in Round Form for longer than about thirty minutes to an hour. And the younger the Pilla, the shorter time they could last in Round Form. And it was pretty hard to pilot a spaceship if all you could do was roll around.

But what the most nonviolent race in the galaxy had been doing since the first hints – decades prior – that the Diamante Families were getting uppity had come to them, was creating gigantic, generational, self-sustaining spaceships.

A Pillar Colony consisted of six generational ships, tethered together. The Pillar had put their entire race into these Colonies and sent them out, each one going in a different direction in space. No one knew how many Colonies had left Pilla, though – based on the Pilla reproductive cycle, which was short; the Pilla lifecycle, which was also relatively short; and the restrictions a generational ship put onto any race – a conservative estimate was a thousand Colonies.

In a sane galaxy, that would have been the end of it. The Pillars would be heading off to nowhere, and the Diamante Families would have been satisfied with destroying their home world. But this wasn't a sane galaxy, and hadn't been since the first Diamante decided that everyone else was a lesser being than he was.

"It's helping, Fren," Roy said, voice tight. "Hold it as long as you can, I think we're almost out of the wreckage."

The ship was still flipping and spinning and it was still unpleasant. Despite the telekinetic shield, we took several more hits, but they were much fewer than we'd had before and all patched quickly. However, we had no banter and no one bothered to even share that things were patched. Some to avoid disturbing Roy and Dr. Wufren – since the telekinesis he was doing was extremely challenging. Some because of the horror of what we'd stumbled into.

But finally everything stopped – the ship flipping around, the pinggggs, and, based on hearing Dr. Wufren, Roy, and Doven all exhale at the same time, the telekinesis and the danger.

"We're floating above it, but we're going to have to move on, soon," Roy said. "But you can all untether and take a look. We need to verify that all windows are intact anyway."

"Sensors indicate they are," Doven added. "But under the circumstances, use extreme caution."

I was sure no one really wanted to look. But at the same time, we needed to. Every room in Quarters had a porthole – and every porthole was space-strength reinforced glass, with an interior sliding and locking metal door. The door meant that if any debris hit and cracked or shattered the glass, it wouldn't cause decompression and death. At least, not at the time of impact.

If sensors were wrong, however – and they could have been damaged due to what we'd just been through – then we could open a porthole door and be sucked out into space, or at least have our faces sucked out, which was just as bad. Hull repair was a lot easier, faster, and far more effective than glass repair.

We had options, but the fastest was to let Bullfrog verify the portholes' integrity. Polliwogs looked like giant frogs, were strong, fast, and could close their nostrils and still breathe. His scales gave him the most natural protection, too.

I shifted into Polliwog form and went with him as backup. Ciarissa manned the doors, as in, closed and locked them from the outside until we could verify that each porthole was secure.

We had ten rooms to do. I was able to avoid looking for the first two. But when we verified the third porthole, I had an excellent view of what Roy had likely thought was the big asteroid. One of our ship's external lights was shining on it – it was easy to see why Roy had made the mistake – the large piece of wreckage was more rounded than angular, with pockets and depressions all over it.

"What part of the ship do you think it...was?" I asked Bullfrog.

"No idea."

"I have run scans," Doven said over the com. "I believe that is a Pillar Birthing Sac."

"I still sense no minds," Ciarissa said quickly.

"We have to go and see if there are any survivors."

"DeeDee, Bullfrog, finish verifying the ship's integrity." Roy's voice was calm.

"We will. But we are going to look for survivors immediately after."

No one argued with me. Bullfrog and I worked our way through the rest of Quarters quickly.

"All portholes secure," Bullfrog said as he, Ciarissa, and I headed to the galley. The others were already there, Roy and Doven arriving when we did.

"I want to search. Now."

"How are we going to search for survivors?" Kyle asked. "We barely made it out as it was."

"I don't care."

Roy put his arm around me. "I know. But if Ciarissa can't feel minds, then there are no survivors."

"If they're in suspended animation, they may not register."

"DeeDee is correct," Ciarissa admitted. "I would sense brainwaves, but if they aren't in a dream state, perhaps not."

"Before we do anything, we need to face one important fact," Willy said. He was one of those men who just got a little leaner and more lived-in looking the older he got. He was worried – I could tell because when he was worried he sucked his cheeks in and his face looked even older and more sunken. "There's only one thing that could and would destroy a Pillar Colony, and it's a Diamante Cruiser or Fleet. Meaning our enemies are close by."

"No," Ciarissa said. "I sense no minds other than ours. Believe me, I have searched for Diamante minds. There are none in the vicinity."

"Based on the wreckage and how close together the debris is, I believe the attack happened a galactic hour ago, no more than three," Doven said.

"So there's a chance there could be survivors."

"We can't destroy ourselves trying to determine that," Roy said gently. "I can't risk this ship and every life on it for what could be nothing."

"But –"

"Our lives for a bug's life isn't a good trade," Willy said. Most Old Earthers had issues with the Pillar, much more than they did with the Arachnidans. Willy said it was because Old Earthers had fear and respect for spiders and none at all for pill bugs, even giant ones.

"Willy's right," Roy said, a little more firmly. "We have a duty to more than ourselves, DeeDee."

"Is now really the time for the Martian Alliance Speech, bro?" Kyle asked. But quietly.

"The Pillar were part of the original Alliance," Tresia pointed out.

"I don't care," Roy said, turning stubborn. "The likelihood of survivors is slim to none and everyone on this ship has too much value to risk."

"Every life has value," I protested, as I tried to keep myself from getting angry, even though Roy and Willy both looked like they were going to start crossing their arms over their chests and begin lectures on which races were more superior than others. "And the Pillar are more than just bugs, Willy, and you know it. You, too, Roy. We can't leave without at least checking for proof of life. We just can't –"

"I may have a way," Dr. Wufren interrupted my protest and whatever counters both Roy and Willy's open mouths were about to utter. "The wreckage is moving, after all. Roy, my boy, if you can match course with it, I could perhaps give it a shove, so as to move it away from the rest of the debris more quickly."

Roy and Doven exchanged a look. "It's workable," Doven said. "But the push would need to be strong in order to allow us to search within a reasonable timeframe to have a hope of rescuing survivors."

"But will it exhaust you?" Roy asked Dr. Wufren. "You've already expended more tele-talent than we'd expected to have to."

Who gave me a very understanding smile. "Some things are worth the risk."

Willy heaved a resigned sigh as Roy looked at me. "Fine. Fren, if you're up for it, let's do it."

"While you all prepare and proceed," Tresia said, "I will suit up."

Everyone stared at her. "Excuse me?" Roy asked finally.

She sighed. "Someone will need to exit the ship to search for survivors. If there are any, the crew member who can grab and carry the most is me. We all have spacesuits, Roy. Were you thinking I would never use mine?"

"She's right, no time for arguing, since the longer we delay, the less likely any survivors will still be alive. I'll help Tresia into her suit." I pulled away from Roy and hugged Dr. Wufren. "Thank you."

Roy looked like he wanted to argue, but apparently my expression told him that discretion was absolutely the better part of valor right now. He, Doven, and Dr. Wufren headed to the cockpit, while Tresia and I headed to where our off-ship gear was stowed.

Unlike Polliskins, which were skintight and literally hell to get on, spacesuits were far more roomy. Getting eight limbs into the suit still required assistance, of course, but nothing like a Polliskin would have.

"Rest assured, DeeDee, I will search diligently."

"I know you will," I said as I did the double-check on her oxygen tanks. "And I'll be there to help you." I stepped into my own suit.

Because I was an extremely strong and talented shifter, I had the advantage of being able to shift my clothing as I shifted my body. This included my space suit. I didn't shift the suit often – it was too important a piece of equipment to risk over-stressing, but in times of need, I could take the risk. And this was a time of need.

"Are you sure you want to accompany me?" she asked as she double-checked my tanks after I'd shifted into Arachnidan form.

"Yes. Because sixteen hands are better than eight, and because someone needs to have your back."

Tresia attached my lifeline and I attached hers – threaded twice through a reinforced belt around our middles, clipped in four places on the suit as well. We tested their holds several times. Then we tested the clips at the ends to make sure they were sound, strong, and not going to come undone.

The rest of the coiled, strong yet supple metal lines were heavy, though it was easier to carry them in this form than it would have been in my natural one. We'd taken the longest lines available to us, meaning we had a good hundred yards of line each.

We went to the airlock, advised the cockpit that we were in position, closed the door tightly behind us, and put our helmets on. We verified that our helmets were tight, that our air and suit pressure was correct, and then we waited. There was a porthole on the external door and, after I verified that it had no damage, we both looked out.

"I can just see the Birthing Sac," Tresia said. "It seems quite...exposed. DeeDee, you must accept that there may indeed be no survivors."

"I know."

"Logically, yes. Emotionally, you see the Pillar as being like you, like the Seraphin. And so you are far more emotionally upset than if this were, say, a

Polliship. And you *want* to find survivors. I understand the desire."

"No. The Pillar are nothing like the Seraphin. As much as I despise the Diamante Families for destroying my people, I can understand why they felt we were a threat. Roy and Kyle? They represent the return to the old ways and destruction of the Diamante Families' rule. I can look at everyone on this ship and explain why our people were destroyed, curtailed, or controlled. But the Pillar? They are a threat to no one. They're a defenseless race that have been persecuted by the Diamante Families for no reason."

"There is always a reason."

"Is there? I could even understand it if the Diamante Families wanted their generational ships. But they don't. They did their best to turn this Colony into dust. And why? Viciousness is the only reason I can come up with. And refuse – I just *refuse* – to allow them to destroy the Pillar like they destroyed my people."

"Looks like the doctor's gotten your target moved away from the majority of the debris and we'll be in position shortly," Roy said over the intercom. "DeeDee, I know without asking that you're in there with Tresia. And I also know without asking that you're in her form. I'll save us the energy and not get into the fight we should be having about this. But are you sure it's wise to go out as an Arachnidan?"

"The body's the thing, Roy, and a stronger body with many more limbs is the thing for this mission. It's good to know you were eavesdropping. And don't worry, we'll be fine."

"Oh, of course I'm not going to worry. Ha ha ha. I just have a quarter of my crew about to risk themselves in the midst of destruction that almost took out my ship. Absolutely nothing to worry about in this scenario. And of course I was listening. It's my ship, you're my crew, and I don't want you doing something reckless out of anger. You're hiding it well, at least you think you are, but I could feel the righteous rage when I was next to you and I can hear it in your voice. Though racing off recklessly is exactly what you're doing."

"We are in position," Doven said. "Airlock will be opening in ten seconds."

"You two can still change your minds," Roy said, as Doven counted down.

Bit back the first several things I wanted to say to this. Willy being unsupportive was one thing. But Roy being hesitant to try to save survivors wasn't sitting well with me at all. "Thanks for the offer. We'll scream if we need you." Tresia and I held on tightly to the bars that were on the sides and top of the doorway.

"Tresia, be safe. DeeDee, I love you."

"Doors opening," Doven said calmly. "Fly straight and true." This was a Quillian blessing, always given when someone was attempting something very dangerous. Nice to get two votes of confidence from the cockpit.

The gravity drive turned off in the airlock, the chamber decompressed, and the door opened. There was the usual pull trying to drag us through the doorway, but we held on as the feeling of weightlessness hit and we began to float. Then Tresia moved slowly through the doorway, still holding onto the bars. She grasped the metal ladder attached to the outside of the *Hummingbird*, and clambered out. I waited for a few seconds, then followed her out in the same way.

We climbed the ladder until we reached the strong metal ring where we attached our lifelines. Tested each clip's hold more than once. We were secure.

Dr. Wufren had done a good job – we were much farther from the main wreckage point than we had been, and there was little floating around the remains of the Birthing Sac.

"I will go first," Tresia said, her voice sounding funny through the helmet's radio system. "You remain here until I have made contact – if I aim incorrectly or have issues, it will be easier for you to pull me back."

"Roger that." We still used Old Earth lingo for certain things. Willy's influence.

I took hold of Tresia's lifeline. She aimed herself and shoved off. I let the lifeline play out, ready to stop it and pull her back if necessary. After a few long seconds, she reached the edge of the damaged Birthing Sac and grabbed on. "I am secure. Searching for signs of life now."

She crawled over what she could of the remains of the ship, humming softly. "I need more line, to continue to search," she said finally.

"Debris is still coming towards you," Roy's voice crackled in our helmets. "Search quickly or come back."

"I can extend using my line," I suggested.

"No, that's too dangerous right now," Roy said, voice tight. "Both of you get back in here."

Someone tapped me on the shoulder. I jumped and shrieked. The being who'd tapped me grabbed a limb and pulled me back to the ship. "Sorry, DeeDee," Dr.

Wufren said. "Thought I could do more out here with the two of you."

"I'm happy I had a tight grasp," Tresia said. "DeeDee's scream almost caused me to lose my hold."

"Why is my ship's doctor also outside of my ship?" Roy asked. "Actually, answer this first – how did my ship's doctor *get* out of my ship?"

"DeeDee and Tresia needed help, bro," Kyle said. "And we figured you'd yell if I was the one to go out to help them."

"Fantastic. Did you all decide we're a democracy all of a sudden?"

I could see part of Dr. Wufren's face through his helmet, and I was pretty sure his watery blue eyes were twinkling. Apparently Tresia wasn't the only one who wasn't seeing enough action. "No, my boy. I just believe that I can assist more effectively from here." He connected his lifeline to the same metal ring as Tresia's and mine. "Tresia, my dear, hold on, please. Roy, I'm going to try to bring the wreckage closer to us. If you could oblige…"

"The three of you are insane. I just want to point this out. Fine. I'm going to move forward, Fren, at the slowest propulsion we have, short bursts only. That's still going to seem fast for the three of you. I want everyone holding on and screaming if you come loose."

"I'm ready," Dr. Wufren said. Tresia and I chimed in with our preparedness.

The *Hummingbird* moved. It felt very different being outside of the ship and the gravity generators, but not as bad as I'd been expecting. I could tell that we were lining up more closely with the wreckage in part because Tresia's lifeline had more slack in it than before.

She moved over parts of the wreckage she hadn't been able to reach prior, as Dr. Wufren sagged. "You need to go back in," I told him.

"Wait!" Tresia called. "I think I've found something!"

"Grab whoever or whatever quickly," Roy said, sounding tenser than he had yet. "Ciarissa's feeling minds. Minds that don't like us."

I didn't hesitate. I shoved off, aiming for where Tresia was. I'd pushed off much harder than she had, and I reached her quickly. I spun while I floated so that I hit the wreckage feet first. My impact caused the wreckage to float farther from the ship, and I heard Roy muttering through the radio.

We stopped moving, meaning Dr. Wufren had probably done something.

"There," Tresia pointed towards the middle. The hole was large enough for us to climb into, so we did.

The interior looked like I'd heard honeycombs described – a series of small, interconnected chambers. Unfortunately, most of those chambers were destroyed. But not all.

There was a section of this Birthing Sac that was still intact. A dozen of the sections sat there, seemingly fine. And each one held what looked like a silver ball about the size of a dinner plate in diameter.

"We have a dozen young, and I think they're all alive," I said.

"I have no idea how we remove them safely," Tresia shared. "Do you?"

"No clue at all. Roy, any guesses from anyone else?"

"No, but we have to get out of here." Roy sighed. "And, I have to say this now – if we take them on board, we can't go to warp. Meaning that the enemies coming are going to be able to overtake us without issue."

"They're protected by something in here – they survived the attack. I think they could handle a short warp jump if we can get them out of the wreckage safely."

"And if they can't?" Roy asked. "Then we killed them, as much as the Diamante Families did."

"I believe I may have the solution thanks to Kyle and Willy," Dr. Wufren said as he climbed into the area we were, a laser cutter in his hands. "If we can cut around the intact chambers, we'll have a smaller and much more manageable portion to work with."

I took the laser cutter from him and started slicing carefully while Willy gave me some tips to avoid cutting through something important, or our suits and tethers, and Roy muttered about a crew who all acted like independent entities instead of functioning like a team.

I chose not to point out that we were actually functioning like a great team, in part because I knew he knew that already, and in other part because I wasn't out here to banter – I was out here to save the remnants of a sentient race.

"Faster would be better," Roy shared after I'd been cutting and he'd been muttering for about five minutes.

"Working on it. The extra pressure isn't helping, in case you weren't sure."

"The Diamante ship will be upon us within ten galactic minutes," Ciarissa said serenely.

"DeeDee, I'm ordering you and the others back to the ship."

"And I'm insubordinate, because I'm not leaving these Pillar here. Period. You can detach my line from the ship and I'll stay here. Come back for me when you can. But they either come with us or I stay with them."

I'd kept on cutting while I said this. I was fairly sure I almost had the section safely removed.

"I feel that DeeDee will need assistance," Tresia said. "Because once we have cut out these young we will have to also cut our way out of this section. So I am also going to stay out, Roy."

"I as well, my boy."

"Have all of you forgotten the motto that's it's better to live to fight another day?" Roy sounded upset and resigned, and I could hear fear there, too, though he was hiding it well. "We're going to give the Diamante Families a great two for one special in a very short while. And, frankly, this isn't how I envisioned any of us going."

"They've never seen our actual ship, you know," I reminded him as I concentrated on cutting through what appeared to be both a very strong beam and a delicate area both. The Pillar designed amazing ships – who would want to destroy this? "As far as whoever will know, we're just a ship trying to salvage at the destruction area."

No one mentioned that the Diamante Families didn't like scavengers unless they were Diamante Family scavengers, which was all of us choosing to ignore the scary situation I was keeping us in

"A good point, DeeDee," Doven said, excitedly. "I have not been thinking, but I may have a solution. It will only work for a short while, however."

"A short while is all we'll have," Roy said. "And, yeah, I think I know what you're planning and I should have thought of it, too."

"Apologize later," Tresia said. "What is the plan and what do we out here do to ensure it succeeds?"

"Doven, I see what you plan," Ciarissa said. "I can assist. However, unless the three of you outside the ship can return within the next minute, you will not be able to return until or unless the Diamante cruiser that's about to enter our space leaves."

"And you'll have to maintain radio silence, too," Roy said tightly. "Meaning if you run into problems, we won't know."

As he said this I heard Dr. Wufren chuckle and realized he'd moved to the hole we'd crawled through. "Yes, we all should have thought of this. Horror makes decent minds a little slower, children, that's all." He returned, still chuckling.

I was getting tired and nudged Tresia. She took the laser cutter from me and continued the work I'd started. My turn to go take a look at the ship. And, as I did so, I just managed not to say the same as everyone else – we all should have thought of this already.

A Quillian with Shaman Powers was able to alter the look of any ship they were in. And Doven was the best of them – at least, per Doven himself, the best of those still left alive. However, even if the best Quillian Shaman returned from the dead, I'd put Doven up against them in terms of skill. If it flew, Doven could alter its shape and appearance at any time and in any way.

Of course, this time, Doven had really outdone himself.

He'd altered the *Hummingbird* to look just like a Diamante Cruiser.

I had no idea how long Doven could hold this apparition, nor did I know what Ciarissa was doing to shield our minds telepathically while also giving any nearby telepaths the idea that we were Diamante crew. But now that we'd all gotten back with the program we ran regularly, I just knew that's what they were doing.

Whether or not it would work was the big question.

I went back to find that Tresia had almost finished cutting out the Birthing Sac. We'd left a lot of space between what I hoped were still intact chambers and living Pillar young and where we'd sliced through the remains of the ship holding them, so if there was something we couldn't see that kept these chambers safe we wouldn't harm it.

There was still plenty of ship between our almost removed section and the exterior remains of the hull. Meaning Tresia was right – we were going to have to cut our way out of here, one way or the other.

As Ciarissa whispered, "*Silence, they are here,*" in all our minds, Tresia made the last freeing cut. Dr. Wufren and I grabbed hold of the now floating Birthing Sac while Tresia turned off the laser cutter and hooked it over one of her arms. Then she also took hold of the Sac.

As far as I could tell, the Pillar inside were still alive and in some form of stasis. Of course, I wasn't the ship's doctor, or a doctor of any kind, so my opinion was more hope than science. And unless our gambit worked, we were all going to be spaced, literally and figuratively, anyway.

As the last of my kind I probably should have been more willing to leave and protect myself. And I might have been able to be coerced, possibly anyway, if Willy and Roy hadn't made me angry.

We passed some hand signals to each other, Tresia went to have her look at what Doven was superimposing over our ship, then she came back and I went to look again. In part because I felt it was better to face my fear, and now that the Pillar were technically in our possession and we couldn't go back to the ship, I was afraid

As I watched the real Diamante Cruiser move into our part of space, it occurred to me that Willy was rarely this overtly anti helping any race that was a Diamante target. And Roy knew me very well, and therefore wasn't likely to make me angry unintentionally, especially over saving innocent lives. Meaning they'd made me angry on purpose, and probably Tresia, too, so that we'd do exactly what we had.

So maybe Roy and Willy had wanted us to save these Pillar as much as I had. Which raised a very key question – why had Willy been openly against this recuse and why had Roy resisted it at all?

This was an unsettling question, because Tresia, Dr. Wufren, and I had no chance if the Diamante personnel chose to attack. We were tethered to the Hummingbird, meaning that if Roy flew off, let alone went to warp, we were dead. If they cut our lines to be able to take off without dragging us along, we were also dead. And Kyle was obviously working the airlock, meaning he was probably in a spacesuit and therefore in a position to cut us all free. For all I knew, Willy was in a suit, too, and also ready to cut us loose.

Why I was even thinking this I couldn't say. I trusted Roy, and everyone else on the *Hummingbird*, with more than my life – I trusted them with everything I was, with the truth of all that I was. We all did. And Roy had as much to lose as the rest of us. More, really. So, why was he resistant, or pretending to be resistant, to save these Pillar and why was I suddenly suspicious of his motives?

Roy was speaking. "Diamante Ship Thirty-three-fifteen." Presumably he was replying to the real Diamante communications officer, and hopefully Ciarissa was feeding him the correct information needed.

Back to worrying. Why hadn't Doven come up with this plan sooner? Why hadn't any of us? Horror and grief could be answers, but were they? Was someone affecting us? Ciarissa certainly had the telepathic skill to do so. But, as with the others, why would she? And why was I no longer trusting her, when we'd just gone through one of the most bonding experiences we could have when we'd been on Polliworld?

Roy shared something innocuous with whoever he was chatting with. Then onto the things that could mean we were dead. "Team searching for survivors. Yes, to destroy them. No, found none."

I was glad we hadn't gotten done faster now. The debris we were in hid the Birthing Sac unless you were looking at it up close, as we'd done. And even if they were using telesights to observe us, they wouldn't see us inside here.

They'd just see our tethers. Going inside somewhere interesting.

Roy and whoever were engaging in more meaningless spacer-typical chatter. More time for me to worry.

How would we get the Pillar somewhere safe? Was Roy right, and would us going to even the shortest warp kill them as surely as the Diamante Families had killed the rest of their kin? Was Willy right? Was a bug's life, even a sentient bug, even a dozen of them, worth more than ours? And even if they survived the warp jump, what? Were we going to dump them off somewhere? Where in the galaxy would they be safe? And who knew how to raise Pillar young anyway?

Who would protect them? Who would love them?

And suddenly, I realized why the Diamante Families wanted this race destroyed.

Of course, that knowledge didn't make waiting easier. Only, in a way, it did. Because I now knew why I was afraid, and I was able to counter it. By reliving my memories, starting from the first time I'd met Roy, up through the last couple of jobs we'd just done. I wondered if Tresia and Dr. Wufren were doing the same, and figured they probably were.

This took some time, but we certainly had it - the cruiser wasn't going anywhere fast. However, they also weren't sending out scout ships or blasting the *Hummingbird* from the sky, so I chose to believe things were going well. I just hoped the cruiser didn't have any kind of telepath on board, though they were required, by their own laws, to advise any other ship, Diamante or otherwise, if they had an Espen working on their ship. One of the many Diamante laws we tended to ignore but, for whatever reason, they usually didn't.

Finally Roy said, "Roger that, over and out." The cruiser took off slowly, not going to warp, but not searching around, either.

The three of us remained quiet - just because the cruiser appeared to be leaving didn't mean it wasn't some kind of a trap or trick. But it continued on until I couldn't see it anymore.

"*All clear,*" Ciarissa said in our minds. "*Doven will keep the illusion in place, just in case. Advise when you are unable to navigate properly and only then will he remove it.*"

"They just went to warp," Roy said. "Get out of there and back into the ship immediately. Faster if you can manage it."

Tresia flipped the laser cutter up and cut away the part of the chamber that we'd crawled through. This took longer than any of us would have liked, but she had to be careful not to cut our tethers or get them caught up in the debris, and Dr. Wufren and I had to keep a hold of the Birthing Sac with the young in it.

"Last piece is away," Tresia said as she once again hooked the laser cutter over her arm. "Shall we return?" she asked me and Dr. Wufren.

"Why wouldn't you?" Roy asked, sounding testy.

"Because we've had an emotional time out here," I replied. I had to figure the others had been treated to the same emotional stress that I had, because it made more sense that they would than not.

Tresia and Dr. Wufren both turned to me. "You, too?" the Doctor asked me. Always nice to be right.

"Yes. Tresia?"

"Oh, yes. Ciarissa, did you pick up anything from any of us?"

"No," Ciarissa replied. "You three were all amazingly quiet, both audibly and telepathically."

"Yeah, well, as to that, we have a situation." Which we'll handle, I thought to myself. And we'll handle it in such a way that our new charges will not be harmed or deserted. "Ciarissa, did you hear what I just thought?"

"No, DeeDee, I did not, but I was not monitoring, either. I am...rather tired."

"I'm sure. The rest of you on the ship, were any of you worried about things?"

"Well, yeah," Kyle said, sounding confused. "You three were outside of the ship when we needed to run. Doven and Ciarissa were extending their powers for a long period of time and big bro was faking it like he'd spent his life in a Diamante uniform. Of course we were worried." The others chimed in with similar concerns.

"We were here, with them," Dr. Wufren said. "We three risked all to get them. That's why they focused on us."

"Plus they, like we, were hiding," Tresia pointed out.

"Who are you talking about?" Roy asked.

"Tell you once we're all on board. We have a dozen Pillar young, by the way. While the three of us are maneuvering back into the bosom of our home, the rest of you try to come up with how we protect them at warp speed. Even if it's a crazy idea, we're going to want to hear it when we're back."

"We will need to go into the cargo hold," Tresia added. "The section of Birthing Sac we have is too large to go through the regular hatch."

"Of course it is," Roy muttered.

"I'll handle it, bro," Kyle said.

"I'll help," Bullfrog said. "Getting into my suit now."

Getting back to the ship wasn't as hard as I'd been worried it would be – we ensured we had firm holds on the Birthing Sac, Doven altered his illusion so that we could see the real cargo hold, we aimed for the belly of the ship, pushed off at the same time, and floated towards our goal.

There were a few pieces of debris floating in our way, but Dr. Wufren managed to shove them away telekinetically, and we avoided minor unpleasant encounters on the way back.

We'd aimed well, and the hold door opened as we got close. Bullfrog and Kyle were tethered to the inside of the ship and they shoved off to catch us. Once they had holds on the Sac, Willy mechanically rewound their tethers and pulled them and our precious cargo back into the ship.

The three of us who'd gone out of the airlock now pulled ourselves back via our tethers, reached the ladder, unclipped, and went back inside. I went last, and as the airlock door closed behind me I heard a group sigh of relief on the com.

"Get out of the suits and to stations as fast as you can," Roy said. "We can't warp out of here, so I want to leave as soon as possible."

"I have an idea," Kyle said as he flooded the airlock with oxygen and let the three of us fully back into the ship.

"And what is that?" Roy asked, patience clearly forced.

"Polliskins inside of space suits," Kyle said, as he helped us get our spacesuits off. "If we can get the babies into Polliskins, then into a space suit, they can probably manage warp. We could even try putting them just into the Polliskin helmets."

"And you think, in the entire history of the Pillar race, that not one of them ever thought of that?" Roy asked.

Bullfrog joined us. "Maybe not, Roy. It would be a rare Polliwog who would have been interested in them prior to the Purge. And I don't think they were frequent visitors to Polliworld."

"They look like your people's idea of food," I pointed out. "I'd be willing to bet that it would have to have been a rare Pillar who wanted to risk getting eaten just to visit somewhere new."

"We must ensure these survive," Tresia said.

Dr. Wufren nodded. "However, Kyle's idea is sound. And one that, frankly, only someone who traveled with a Polliwog and visited Polliworld regularly would think of."

"I like the kid's idea, but I have a question – how will we get them into the suits without crushing them?" Willy asked. "Because the helmet idea won't work."

"We'll have them stay in Round Form," I answered. "I have a plan as well. Besides, they're willing to take the risk. Now that they know for sure that we're trying to save them, that is."

There was silence on the com, and the expressions on Kyle, Willy, and Bullfrog's faces shared that they felt I'd finally gone around the comets once too many times. Tresia and Dr. Wufren, on the other hand, looked unsurprised and also determined.

"Group meeting, in the hold," Dr. Wufren said. "DeeDee, Tresia, and I have something to tell the rest of you."

"We will complete two tasks at the same time," Tresia added, "and get our young survivors set up to survive their rescue."

The six of us gathered all of our Polliskins and met up with Roy, Doven, and Ciarissa in the cargo hold. Roy looked worried and unhappy. "Tell me again why we're not trying to get out of here and why my entire crew is being insubordinate?"

"It was a test," I said, as I looked at the Pillar still sleeping in their Sacs. The last ones from this colony. "They wanted to be sure they could trust us."

"They who?" Willy asked.

"The Pillar. These Pillar. I know why the Diamante Families destroyed Pilla and why they want to kill every last Pillar left."

Ciarissa cocked her head. Her blonde hair floated around her - our gravity generators were working, this was just the way Ciarissa's hair was most of the time. I didn't know enough Espens to know if this was common or not with their telepaths. For all I knew, her hair floated because she was near a telekinetic, or Dr. Wufren used her hair for practice. It was one of those questions I'd never felt comfortable asking.

"They're telepathic," she said softly. Tresia, Dr. Wufren, and I nodded. "But not individually and not when they're awake. It only happens when they're young and in these chambers. The Birthing Sacs...amplify their talents."

"So does proximity to each other."

Roy shook his head. "How could that be and no one knew about it?"

"And why can't we hear them -" Kyle stopped speaking abruptly. "Oh."

"They're talking to you?" Tresia asked him.

He nodded. "Kind of. Not like Ciarissa does. It's more like...I'm feeling what they want me to."

"Yes, that's what it was like for me," Tresia said.

"Me, too."

"I as well, but, Roy to answer your question, why share a power that your young possess?" Dr. Wufren asked. "Someone realized it, and the moment they did..."

"They were slaughtered," I finished. "I assume the young Pillars who were in Birthing Sacs at the time were the ones who sounded the alarm to leave Pilla in the first place."

Ciarissa nodded. "There were some...Espens who warned Pilla of the danger, but by the time that warning came, they were already making preparations to leave their planet."

There was an Espen underground set up across the galaxy – I'd learned that during our last mission. That they'd warned Pilla made sense. That Pilla had already known should have raised some questions, though.

"If Espens knew the Pillar were aware of the danger, how is it that this telepathic talent was not known by the entire galaxy?" Doven asked.

Ciarissa shook her head. "Espen's leaders were firmly on the path of neutrality. The assumption, encouraged by Pillar leadership, by the way, was that they'd been warned by someone else."

"They had been." I pointed to the Birthing Sac. "By their children. And I'm sure they lied because they knew why the Diamante Families wanted to destroy them."

"But how did the Diamante families figure it out?" Kyle asked. "If an Espen couldn't tell the babies were telepathic, how did a Diamante manage it?"

"Probably the same way we did," Tresia said. "The Diamante Families visited all the worlds first, before they destroyed them. Perhaps one or more of them felt emotionally manipulated, made the same logical leaps that DeeDee, Fren, and I did, and then reported back."

"By the time they were being warned, they would have had their children remain...hidden," Ciarissa added.

"But why would they have shown their power to anyone even remotely connected to the Diamante Families?" Doven asked.

I shrugged. "They were children. Children are curious. Or maybe they were afraid. Or excited. It doesn't matter why – it matters that there is a reason, a real reason, why the Diamante Families are trying to destroy this race."

"Why, though?" Roy asked. "Based on the little we know, they aren't as powerful as an average Espen, and the moment they leave their Birthing Sacs they have no more telepathic power. Why hunt them down and leave Espen alone?"

"Espen acquiesced," Ciarissa said sadly. "In order to preserve our world we took oaths and agreed to the tele-restraints and more when we were off-planet."

"And the Pillar did not wish to capitulate to evil," Dr. Wufren said. "Any more than the Seraphin did."

"And the result was the same." I took a deep breath and let it out slowly. "Roy, none of us have acted normally since we spotted the wreckage. You, in particular."

"What do you mean? Because I wanted to get out of here and keep our crew alive?"

"Frankly, yes. And I think you resisted and Willy was species-ist and you both angered me and Tresia enough that we went against your orders because, as I said before, we were all being tested. The Pillar with us are young children. They're curious and, right now, they're very afraid. Horror and devastation cause beings to not think right all the time, as our good doctor mentioned earlier. They wanted to be sure that the beings rescuing them weren't worse than the beings that had destroyed their entire colony."

"I didn't feel emotionally manipulated," Roy protested.

"Me either, and I don't buy it," Willy said. "I think you're all jumping to a heck of a conclusion, little girl."

"I spent most of the time we were hiding from the Diamante Cruiser being afraid. Of Roy, of all of you deserting us. Of other things, things I've never worried about since our first mission together. I firmly believe my emotions were influenced by the Pillar, so they could see if their fears were grounded or not."

Tresia nodded. "I experienced the same – the same fears, and the same reasoning that my fears were groundless."

"I'm not a fan of the Pillar," Willy said. "Don't wish 'em ill, but they were never my favorite aliens. So how did they affect me?"

"I think they just helped you speak out. Note that you still helped rescue them. I don't think they care that you don't want to hang out with them, Willy. I think they care that you're trying to help figure out how to keep them alive, despite not having affinity for their race."

Doven nodded. "It proves you are not like the Diamante Families and their troops."

"That makes sense, but why affect me to not want to search for them?" Roy asked.

"Because the proof of what kind of beings we are was based on that, my boy. What would we do when our captain and leader told us to let them die? What would that captain do when we were insubordinate?"

"Get pissed off," Kyle muttered.

Willy cocked his head. "Yeah, the kid's right. So, Roy was angry with the situation, I wasn't happy, but you three went and helped anyway. Four, really, because Kyle couldn't wait to get a spacesuit on."

"Everyone likes to get in on the action sometimes," I pointed out. Then went on quickly, lest Roy start lecturing Kyle about how he shouldn't risk himself ever. Basically, if Roy could keep his entire crew wrapped up safe and tight and still manage to do the work we needed to, he would. "But are you angry now?"

Roy sighed. "I'd love to say yes, but I'm frankly far more worried than anything else."

"I hear the babies talking, in that sense," Willy said. "They're alive and happy to be so. So, no, I'm not angry."

"I feel them as well," Doven said. "They seem to...like us."

"All of us?" Roy asked a little suspiciously.

"Ask them yourselves," I suggested.

"I don't know how," Roy said. "I don't feel anything different."

Willy barked a laugh. "Roy, if they're talking to me, they'll talk to you."

"Maybe they won't –" Roy jerked. "Oh. That's...different. Are you sure they're telepathic? It feels all emotional to me. They're kind of...hugging me and apologizing for being afraid?"

"Probably they are, yes." I felt the Pillar tell me I was correct.

"Empathy is rare," Ciarissa said, "but not unheard of, and it's definitely a telepathic trait. A specialty, if you will. Most Espens don't focus on emotion manipulation because controlling the mind is more effective."

"Or the body," Dr. Wufren said cheerfully. Then he looked at me and no longer appeared cheerful. "You're going to be the only one capable of doing what must be done."

"I know."

"What do you mean?" Kyle asked. "They're in Round Form. We can get them into one or two Polliskins easily enough, same with the space suit or suits."

"Yes, but that won't be enough. And I don't think we actually want to remove them from the Birthing Sac. However, your idea is still a good one, Kyle." I went and gave Roy a kiss. "Help me get into a Polliskin or six, will you?"

"Why?" he asked, looking worried.

"Because I'm going to shift into something dangerous."

Roy shook his head and hugged me to him. "Why did I know that's what you were going to say?"

"You're smarter than the average spacer."

"Yeah? I don't think that can be proven by anything that's happened in the last couple of hours."

Roy and I both would have liked to have done something more than just get me into a Polliskin, but time was running out and we'd spent more than enough of it explaining what was going on.

Per Willy, Polliskins were like wetsuits from Old Earth, only they were far more adaptable and also good protection for anyone who wasn't a Polliwog who was visiting Polliworld. They were also incredibly hard to get into. Getting more than one on was a challenge of major proportions. Whether the effort would be worthwhile, based on what we wanted the suits to do, was, currently, anyone's guess.

"Why are you willing to die for them?" Roy asked me as we finally got the last suit on. "Because what you're going to do means you're at as much risk as they are. More, really."

I leaned against him. "Because they need someone who loves them."

"That's true of every being, babe."

"Yes, but the Pillar are different from others, in many ways. And one of those ways is that they require the love of others to survive. That's part of why they create music – to spread love."

"You got that from floating around in space for a while?"

"No. I got that from what the Pillar told me emotionally, both while floating around in space and once we were back here."

He sighed and hugged me tightly. "I need you, too, you know. We all do. And not just because of what you can do. But because of who you are, and who you are to us...to me."

I buried my face in his chest. "I know. I feel the same way about you, you know that. But..."

He kissed the top of my head. "But you can never truly have a Seraphin child. And we don't know if we can have children of our own. And there are a dozen children in my cargo hold who need a mother who loves them. I get it, babe. But I don't see it as a long term solution."

I laughed. "Roy, when we met, you said taking me with you was a short term solution. Trust me, we'll manage. We always do."

He kissed me. As always it was amazing, but not as long as either one of us would have liked. Not smart to spend too much time making out when our enemies could be back and in greater numbers.

We went back to the cargo hold. I put on a Polliskin helmet and my spacesuit. Then I shifted.

As a shifter, the form was the thing. You could do whatever your form could, and could not do whatever your form couldn't. But the stronger the shifter, the more options you had in terms of just what your form was going to be.

The strongest beings in the galaxy were the Troglodytes from Rockenroll, because they were literally beings made out of stone. In Round Form a Pillar's shell became like iron, but only for as long as that form could hold out under the stress of warp.

However, a cross between a Troglodyte and a Pillar could, in theory, survive an extended warp. Only there was no such cross, because those two races did not interbreed with each other.

Until now.

The beauty of being a shape shifter of my strength and skill was that I had the ability to become anything I wanted. The danger was that what I wanted might not be something that could, in actual fact, survive existence, even for a short period of time.

I needed my outer shell to be made of Troglodyte stone, the inner shell to be the iron hardness of the Round Form, but the rest of my inside portion to be soft and filled with the fifty little legs of a Pillar, so that I could hold the Birthing Sac and keep it safe and steady. All of which needed to be inside both the six Polliskins I had on and my spacesuit. And I needed to be four times larger than the Pillar actually were and two times larger than the biggest Troglodyte, in order to be large enough to surround this Sac.

And I had no idea if this would work, or if I and the Pillar young with us would die. I only knew that, when faced with watching the last of their colony and, possibly, the last Pillar in the galaxy die, I was willing to risk whatever I had to in order to ensure that didn't happen.

My willingness to risk wasn't based on the Pillar emotionally manipulating me, or on any kind of fatalism. Roy had actually called it correctly when we were alone – I had no idea if I would ever have a child of my own.

Normally, I never thought about this. We were usually too busy trying to stay alive for me to ponder progeny or my lack thereof. And I wouldn't have called myself overly maternal on a normal day.

But this wasn't a normal day.

While I knew the Pillar had connected in some way with everyone on the crew by now, I also knew that they'd connected the most strongly with me. They could have connected to Tresia or Ciarissa, but they'd chosen me, and I knew they had.

Not just because I cared and had risked my life to save them, but because I was the only one who could, at any time I wanted or they needed, become a Pillar. Become their mother, both figuratively and literally.

And I could also become something unheard of, in the hopes of saving them.

The first portion of this experiment worked – both the space suit and my Polliskin layers altered with me and didn't rip or explode off me. So I'd have the protection these offered, and so would the Pillar.

True, I filled most of the hold, but I was functioning. I'd never gone into Pillar form before; there had never been a need. However, we'd visited Rockenroll enough, and being heavy and strong had its advantages, so I'd assumed Troglodyte form many times. Plus I had practice looking like one kind of being on the outside and altering my insides into something else.

I altered next into the Pillar portion of my experimental form, while remaining a Troglodyte at the same time.

Again, I had success. I hadn't destroyed myself or turned into something that couldn't move, function, or think. The Pillar shell was the hardest, but that was one of the reasons I'd put on more than one Polliskin – the outermost Polliskin layer I turned to the iron hardness of the Round Form. My spacesuit altered to Troglodyte stone. If there were still competitions for the most amazing shapes managed – as there had been before the Purge – I'd have been guaranteed to win.

I pointedly didn't pay attention to anyone's expressions, Roy's in particular. There was no way this look was going to fulfill anyone's fantasies. However, I was able to move, albeit slowly, and to curl around the Birthing Sac securely. The Sac's rough edges didn't bother me – I could feel them, but they weren't causing discomfort because my many legs were able to position the Birthing Sac perfectly to hold it steady and not hurt myself at the same time. Plus the Polliskins were a great buffer.

Ciarissa was in my mind – at my request and Roy's insistence. I wasn't sure if I could communicate with anyone properly in this form, and if things were going wrong, the Pillar and I would have only seconds.

"I am here, DeeDee," she said soothingly. "I am connected to you and the children as well."

"Are you too tired?"

"Not for this."

I could feel straps being put on and around me – to keep me stationary during flight and most importantly during warp.

"It's almost time," Ciarissa said. "Do you need one of us to stay in the hold with you?"

"Absolutely not. But please ask Bullfrog to stay close." If I was in danger, he'd get to me fastest and was the strongest and so the most likely to be able to help open me up. So to speak.

"He is indeed staying near. But all will be well, DeeDee. Fren is also monitoring and will use his powers as necessary."

The entire crew was going to be drained if this succeeded. And if it did succeed, we'd need to hope we could get to someplace calm where we could recuperate. But first we had to make it.

I could tell when we made the jump to warp because I could feel the extra pressure pushing against my outer shells. But it didn't bother me any more than warp normally did. And, for once, I couldn't really see the suffocating blackness that accompanied warp, because in Round Form my face was tucked down and inside the outer shell. As a matter of fact, my face was resting against the Birthing Sac.

So when the children began to sing, I heard it clearly.

Pillar music was their gift to the galaxy, but this was different. It wasn't just music or sound, it was feeling and thoughts and history. All the history of the Pillar race. All of their race, each and every one of them who had ever existed since the first Pillar became sentient.

Everything every Pillar had ever seen or experienced was in this song, and it was being passed to me. Because the children knew the risk we were taking and, if they died, they wanted someone to remember them and to sing their song. Someone they loved.

As the song washed over me and burrowed into my mind, I realized I could only hear it as I was in this form and in this way. But all the Pillar's music, every song any of us had ever heard, was simply a section of this one song. The Song of Life.

The Song was beautiful and, in some ways, terrible, all-encompassing and overwhelming, and yet also sublime and wonderful. The Pillar lived short individual lives, but the lifespan of their race was long, and as long as the Song existed, the Pillar existed as well. So long as the Song was sung, the Pillar lived. When the Song stopped, so would their race.

And now I knew the Song, and Ciarissa probably did as well. Two of us out of the billions of beings in the galaxy. But two was better than none. Two could share the Song with others.

But I didn't want us to be the last ones to know the Song. I wanted the children who were singing the Song to me to continue on. To have their own children who would learn the Song and carry it on down throughout the generations. Because they loved me and I now loved them – for trusting me, for sharing their Song with me, for needing me in a way no one else ever had before.

They knew this, and that was why they shared the Song with me. Because I wanted for them what any mother would – for them to live and prosper and go on forever.

The pressure on my outermost shell was more intense for a moment, and then it stopped. I felt the straps being loosened.

"We are in orbit around Rockenroll, DeeDee," Ciarissa said in my mind. *"Kyle's idea worked. Bullfrog is with you. Willy has friends on the planet who he thinks will be able to effectively hide, protect, and raise the Pillar children...and ensure their song continues."*

I moved slowly, to be certain that I didn't jostle the Birthing Sac. Once the Sac was safely away from me, I shifted back to my regular form.

Bullfrog coughed. "Uh, DeeDee?"

"Yes?" My voice sounded funny. Higher pitched and more musical.

"You're, ah, not really back. To you, I mean."

I looked down. Among other things, I still had fifty limbs. "Oh. Uh...whoops."

"I could be wrong, but I don't think this is the look Roy's hoping you use for every day."

"You think not? Really?" As I shifted back to me, to DeeDee Daniels from Seraphina, not from Pilla, I could hear the children in my head. They were laughing and adding to the Song – so that future generations would know that there were some beings out there who would indeed love them, no matter what form they were in.

The Song of Life bound me to them. I now knew the Song, knew how to sing it. I would sing it, over and over again, aloud and to myself. And I knew one other thing – the Pillar's telepathy wasn't why the Diamante Families wanted them destroyed.

What the Diamante Families feared was the Song. Because somewhere in the Song was the key to defeating them. And if I sang the Song long enough, I'd figure out what that was.

✈ About the Author ✈

Gini Koch writes the fast, fresh and funny Alien/Katherine "Kitty" Katt series for DAW Books, the Necropolis Enforcement Files series, and the Martian Alliance Chronicles series. Touched by an Alien, Book 1 in the Alien series, was named by Booklist as one of the Top Ten Adult SF/F novels of 2010. Alien in the House, Book 7 in her long-running Alien series, won the RT Book Reviews Reviewer's Choice Award as the Best Futuristic Romance of 2013.

As G.J. Koch she writes the Alexander Outland series and she's made the most of multiple personality disorder by writing under a variety of other pen names as well, including Anita Ensal, Jemma Chase, A.E. Stanton, and J.C. Koch.

A Study in Starlets, the next adventure in Gini's Sherlock Holmes universe, is out now, and she also has stories featured in a variety of anthologies, including the Unidentified Funny Objects 3, Clockwork Universe: Steampunk vs. Aliens, Two Hundred and Twenty-One Baker Streets, Temporally Out of Order, Unidentified Funny Objects 4, and The X-Files: Trust No One anthologies; writing as Anita Ensal, in The Book of Exodi, Love and Rockets, and Boondocks Fantasy anthologies; and, writing as J.C. Koch, in Kaiju Rising: Age of Monsters, The Madness of Cthulhu, Vol. 1, and A Darke Phantastique anthologies, and, coming in

2016, The Mammoth Book of Kaiju, and MECH: Age of Steel anthologies. Gini will also be featured in the Out of Tune 2, WERE-, Alien Artifacts, Unidentified Funny Objects 5, alt. Sherlock Holmes: New Visions of the Great Detective, and Humanity 2.0 anthologies, all coming in 2016.

Reach Gini via her website – www.ginikoch.com

Reach Gini

Her website - http://www.ginikoch.com
The Blah, Blah, Blah Blog -
    http://ginikoch.blogspot.com/
Twitter - @GiniKoch
Facebook - facebook.com/Gini.Koch
Facebook Fan Page: Hairspray & Rock 'n' Roll –
    https://www.facebook.com/GiniKochAuthor
Pinterest – http://www.pinterest.com/ginikoch/
The Official Fan Site of the Alien Collective -
    http://thealiencollectivevirtualhq.blogspot.com/
E-mail - gini@ginikoch.com

Gini Koch Writing As...

Anita Ensal
A CUP OF JOE

Anthologies
LOVE AND ROCKETS – *Wanted*
BOONDOCKS FANTASY – *Being Neighborly*
THE BOOK OF EXODI – *The Last Day on Earth*

G.J. Koch
ALEXANDER OUTLAND: SPACE PIRATE

Jemma Chase
THE DISCIPLE AND OTHER STORIES
OF THE PARANORMAL

J.C. Koch
Anthologies
THE MADNESS OF CTHULHU – *Little Lady*
A DARKE PHANTASTIQUE – *Outsiders*
KAIJU RISING: AGE OF MONSTERS –
With Bright Shining Faces
MECH: AGE OF STEEL – *Jäegermeister* (coming 2016)
THE MAMMOTH BOOK OF KAIJU –
With Bright Shining Faces (coming 2016)

Gini Koch

The Alien/Katherine "Kitty" Katt Series
from DAW Books

Booklist names
TOUCHED BY AN ALIEN
One of the top 10 adult SF/F novels of 2010!

RT Book Reviews Reviewers'
Choice Awards
ALIEN IN THE HOUSE
wins Best Futuristic Romance of 2013!

"If you like your books moving at the speed of sound,
with plenty of action, then look into Gini Koch."
— Fresh Fiction

TOUCHED BY AN ALIEN
978-0-7564-0600-4
Also in audio!

ALIEN TANGO
978-0-7564-0632-5

ALIEN IN CHIEF
978-0-7564-1007-0

CAMP ALIEN
Coming May 2016

ALIEN NATION
Coming December 2016

ALIENS ABROAD
Coming May 2017

"Rollicking, sexy fun – science fiction hasn't been this
much of a blast since…well, never. Grab on with both
hands and
enjoy the wild, lusty ride."
– Robert J. Sawyer,
Hugo Award-winning author of *Triggers*

Gini Koch

The Necropolis Enforcement Files Series

"Gini Koch delivers on the humor, mayhem, and mystery with The Night Beat – this mondo monster noir crackles
with snappy dialogue, great characters, and twists and turns that will keep you guessing."
– Carolyn Crane,
author of The Disillusionists trilogy

"Do you just LOVE the paranormal world? Historical figures? Well The Night Beat is an all you can eat buffet of
creatures that bump, thud, poof, sniff, shamble, or zip in the night!"
– I Smell Sheep

THE NIGHT BEAT
978-1-4776-3138-6

NIGHT MUSIC
Coming 2016

"The fascinating premise of Necroplis City, a place
existing just below Prosaic City (the human location) in
another dimension, that supernatural beings can travel
back
and forth between, enhances the story, and
this reviewer hopes to learn more about
the city itself in book two."
– Bitten By Books

Gini Koch
writing as
Jemma Chase

A time-traveling vampire hunter. The search for the hottest place on Earth. A salvage hunter at the edge of the galaxy. A maze that grows more terrifying with each turn. And someone trapped in a deadly game of hide and seek. What do they have in common? Surprises, thrills, twists, romance, and danger, all within different realms of the paranormal. Strange Protection, Hotter Than Hell, Waiting, Amazing, and The Disciple – for the first time, these five short stories, novelettes, and novellas of the paranormal by Gini Koch writing as Jemma Chase are in one collection. These stories will introduce you to dangers and romance lurking around the corner, and show you the secret worlds and creatures just outside of everyday view. So come and enter the paranormal worlds of Jemma Chase. Just remember to bring a map to lead you back to your normal world, because the writer's web is like a maze, and not all mazes have exits.

THE DISCIPLE
AND OTHER STORIES OF
THE PARANORMAL
978-1-5086-5365-3

Gini Koch
writing as
Anita Ensal

When Emily smiles at David, the Chosen One, as if
he's a normal person, his sheltered existence plunges
into terror and deception, forcing him to see that the
world might not be as perfect as he's always believed.
If the choice is between love or perfection, which would
you choose?

"Smart, unexpected...A Cup of Joe is solid science
fiction with a big dollop of romance and a tasty twist
you won't see coming."
–Marsheila Rockwell,
author of Dungeons & Dragons Online novels *Skein of
Shadows* and *The Shard Axe*

A CUP OF JOE
978-148404-0874

Gini Koch

Welcome to Happy Acres, where the residents, both
living and dead, are always happy to meet new friends,
spark
new romances, and occasionally get rid of odious
relatives.

"...I dearly love a good ghost story, and this one has all
my favorite elements: humor; a strong, likeable
protagonist
and a diverse cast of characters; a dash of romance;
a bit of history; a whiff of horror; the
supernatural, of course; and – hurrah!
– just desserts (with a dash of cinnamon)."
– The Nameless Zine

THE HAPPY ACRES HAUNTED HOTEL FOR ACTIVE SENIORS
978-1-48405-5328

Gini Koch

Want to know the untold story of Gini Koch? Did Gini really spend time in the Peace Corps? And did she really get arrested for stalking Nathan Fillion? Is she fluent in any language other than sarcasm? And what's the real reason she's banned from Denny's? The answer to these and other burning questions are in this book! So what are you waiting for? Buy this book NOW! It's not getting any younger, you know. Is it fact or fiction? You decide.

"I laughed. I laughed until I snorted soda pop out my nose, and my cats ran for cover."
– Word of the Nerd

RANDOM MUSINGS
FROM THE FUNNY GIRL
978-1-4952-4859-7

Gini Koch
writing as
Anita Ensal

BOONDOCKS FANTASY
(anthology from DAW Books)
"Being Neighborly"
978-0-7564-0653-0

LOVE AND ROCKETS
(anthology from DAW Books)
"Wanted"
978-0-7564-0650-9

Gini Koch

The Martian Alliance Chronicles

Join the crew of the Hummingbird as they take on the rich, famous, and sleazy of the galaxy. They're also on a long-term secret mission, so it's a good thing they're the best con artists, spacers, and roughnecks in the Milky Way, because they're going to need all their skills to ensure the Martian Alliance wins the war and saves the day.

THE ROYAL SCAM
978-1-31161-8825
ebook only

THREE CARD MONTE
978-1-31187-9677
ebook only

A BUG'S LIFE
978-1-31001-6950
ebook only

Gini Koch
writing as
G.J. Koch

The Alexander Outland Series
from Night Shade Books

In space, no one can hear you scheme...

"In the grand tradition of Harry Harrison's *Stainless Steel Rat*, G.J. Koch introduces us to Captain Alexander Napoleon Outland and his ribald and vibrant crew taking the universe by storm... A humorous romp with twists and turns aplenty."
– Michael A. Stackpole,
author of *At the Queen's Command* and *Of Limited Loyalty*

"Laugh-out loud, read until you drop, Alexander (the) Outland is my favorite space pirate."
– Patricia Briggs,
author of the Mercy Thompson series

Sometimes piracy just doesn't pay.

ALEXANDER OUTLAND: SPACE PIRATE
978-1-5978-0423-3
Also in audio!

NSB
NIGHT
SHADE
BOOKS

Short Stories
from Gini Koch

CLOCKWORK UNIVERSE:
STEAMPUNK VS. ALIENS
(anthology)
"A Clockwork Alien"
978-1-9407-0900-0

UNIDENTIFIED FUNNY OBJECTS 3
(anthology)
"Live at the Scene"
978-0-9884-3284-0

UNIDENTIFIED FUNNY OBJECTS 4
(anthology)
"Support Your Local Alien"
978-0-9884-3286-4

TWO HUNDRED AND TWENTY-ONE
BAKER STREETS
(anthology)
"All the Single Ladies"
978-1-7810-8222-5

Short Stories from Gini Koch continued...

A STUDY IN STARLETS
B014ROFUNG
ebook only

THE X-FILES: TRUST NO ONE
(anthology)
"Sewers"
978-1-6314-0278-4

TEMPORALLY OUT OF ORDER
(anthology)
"Alien Time Warp"
978-1-9407-0902-4

Short Stories
from Gini Koch
writing as
J.C. Koch

THE MADNESS OF CTHUHLU
VOLUME 1
(anthology)
"Little Lady"
978-1-7811-6452-5

A DARKE PHANTASTIQUE
(anthology)
"Outsiders"
978-0-9841-6765-4

KAIJU RISING: AGE OF MONSTERS
(anthology)
"With Bright Shining Faces"
978-0-9913-6056-7

Made in the USA
Coppell, TX
26 February 2021